AIRPORT NURSE

'She's what we need—highly qualified, not too young and not too attractive.' Sister Virginia Mayhew was furious when she overheard her new boss talking about her. But with such an exciting, demanding job at a busy airport medical centre she was just about prepared to put up with the high-handed, arrogant and impatient Dr Richard Tranter!

Betty Beaty was born in Yorkshire and read Sociology at Leeds University. She has served as a WAAF officer, has flown all over Europe as an air hostess and worked as a medical social worker at two London hospitals and recently in Kent. She is married to David Beaty, the author and aviation psychologist. After living in Canada for some time, from where her husband was then flying the Atlantic, they settled in Kent, a short distance from an airport. They have three daughters, the youngest of whom is a State Registered Nurse. Betty Beaty has written twenty-seven novels, several of them with medical or aviation backgrounds.

For D

AIRPORT NURSE

BY

BETTY BEATY

MILLS & BOON LIMITED
15–16 BROOK'S MEWS
LONDON W1A 1DR

CHAPTER ONE

AT precisely three o'clock on the afternoon of July the eighteenth, Sister Virginia Mayhew drove her ancient Ford estate car on to the road signposted Entwick Airport.

She had no premonition that she was about to do anything more than submit herself for interview at the new airport medical centre.

She was a little nervous, of course. She disliked interviews. But at thirty years and one month old, she had learned how to conceal her nervousness behind firm lips and with her head held high. So far, her journey down from London was going according to her meticulous schedule. The hedges, festooned with early honeysuckle and the white stars of dog-roses, smelled sweet. The car was running well. Sister Mayhew's former fiancé, whom she tried not to think about too much, had once said that she drove her car as she lived, calmly and quietly and with far too much consideration for other people.

The event that followed one minute later would therefore have surprised him as much as it appalled her. Afterwards, she was not even sure exactly what had happened.

She remembered rounding a curve. Then events and impressions seemed to run together. She could remember, on the one side, her eye being captured by the sight of a gigantic red and yellow claw the size of a high-rise block looming over the hedge on her right like a Star Wars honeysuckle. She had just worked out that this monster swinging its head crazily backwards and forwards on its gantry was something to do with radar, when from her left-hand side, out into her path, head down over the handlebars, swooped a cyclist.

Virginia's momentary loss of concentration cost her dearly. She dragged her eyes back to the road, and stood on the brakes. She tried to swing the steering wheel round to the right.

But there was a dreadful thud, a scrape, a crunch of metal, an angry masculine shout, and a brief almost unbearable silence. That it must have been very brief Virginia was sure, because she had barely had time to unstrap herself, let alone put her hand on the door, when it was wrenched open.

A large man in blue denim jeans and short-sleeved denim shirt thrust his head into the car, gave her a quick searching look, and said icily, 'I suggest you get out.'

His voice was not exactly loud, but it had an abrasive quality that decreased her shock and increased her anger. What also increased her anger but which also was a sign of shock was that she noticed the irrelevancy that his eyes were exactly the same blue as his denims, and just about as devoid of feeling.

'You're not hurt, I take it,' he said grimly, the blue eyes travelling over her dispassionately, the straight dark brows drawn together.

'No,' she replied, holding herself very erect, the way over the years she had schooled herself to do, 'but I might well have been. The accident was entirely your fault!'

She had not exactly meant to say that—she was not normally the sort of person who got out of her car accusing a stranger. She did not know what had come over her. The accident must have shocked her profoundly. She watched the stranger walk away and begin to untangle the remains of his bicycle. Carefully he disengaged the spokes. When one seemed intractable he reached into the back pocket of his jeans, brought out a spanner and freed the spoke from the corner of her bumper, all in a silence that was somehow much more disturbingly accusative than her own sharp tones.

'You've only got a slight dent on your bumper,' he said, as if that too were a crime, as he lifted in both hands the buckled frame that was his bike. 'But nevertheless, *let that be a lesson to you*.'

'A lesson to me? Did I hear you say a lesson to *me*?' She followed him over as he lifted the wreckage and laid it unhurriedly on the bank under the hedge.

'I hope you did. I hope you heard correctly.' He straightened and stood regarding her from his impressive height with his muscular mechanic's arms folded across his chest. Virginia was ashamed of noticing how very muscular and sunburned they were. 'Because that's what I said, young woman,' he added.

'As it was not my fault, it can hardly be a lesson,' she heard herself say, her own voice rising edgily, 'And I'm *not* a young woman. I'm thirty years old.'

A gleam of amusement lit the man's blue eyes and deepened the little laughter lines at the corners of his mouth. He inclined his head in a way that she found both irritating and insulting.

'Even such a great age,' he said drily, 'doesn't mean you're a safe driver.'

'But I am!'

'Not to me, young woman!'

'But it was your fault—your fault entirely! You came out of a side road! It was my right of way. I was going steadily along . . .'

'Gazing up at the radar bowl,' he interrupted.

'And out you came from that side road there.' Virginia looked at her watch. Time was hastening by. Though, prudent as always, she had allowed plenty of margin before the interview, she was now impatient to be on her way. 'I shall be happy to give you a lift to wherever you want to go,' she said firmly and with dignity. 'I presume you were making for the airport?'

'I was.'

'Well then, we can put your bike in the back.'

Though her legs felt as weak as a half set jelly she forced herself to walk steadily to the back of the car and lift up the hatch, with dignity and finality.

'I can see,' said the man, 'that this has happened to you before, young woman.'

'Indeed it has not!'

'Never?'

'Never! Let me tell you I have a twelve-year-old clean licence!'

The man smiled mirthlessly. 'You're thirty years old, and you have a twelve-year-old clean licence. But between you and it . . .' He laid the wreckage of his bicycle in the back of the car with a profound care that spoke more loudly and clearly than mere words, then straightened. 'Now, young woman,' he said in a tone that gave her some faint warning that he was about to demolish her. 'Now, young woman, let *me* show *you* something.' He crooked his finger for her to follow him round to the front of the car, then past the bumper with the slight dent, past the passenger door. With an accusing finger he pointed to the road, to where two sets of dotted white lines emerged from under her car. 'Do you know what those are?'

'Of course I do. White lines.'

'Meaning?'

'That *I* was on the minor road.'

'And it was therefore whose right of way?'

'Yours,' she said in a muffled tone that showed the word was strangling her.

'I didn't hear that clearly.'

'Yours,' she repeated loudly.

'Thank you. And therefore the fault was . . .'

'Mine.'

He bowed. 'Thank you.'

It was then that Virginia noticed a jagged cut on his head, just below the line of his reddish-brown hair. A little trickle of blood was running down his temple, and he brushed it aside impatiently. The sight somehow moved her profoundly, and her mood somersaulted.

'Look,' she said in an entirely different tone, 'you're hurt!'

'I'll survive.'

'And I'm very sorry about the accident. It was my fault—mine entirely. I'll see you get a new bike, if you would give me your name and address, and if you're late for work, I'll vouch for you. But in the meantime I would like to have a look at that cut.'

She was indeed sorry, profoundly sorry, and though she had of course been rashly indignant to begin with, most men would have accepted her manifestly sincere apology. But the cyclist backed away as she extended her hand.

'As a matter of fact,' she said very firmly, 'I was on my way to the medical department of Entwick Airport. I can tell you here and now you should have a clean dressing on that, and a tetanus jab. I'm a Nursing Sister.'

The man in blue denims raised an eyebrow.

'You've no doubt been nursing,' he said with deceptive mildness, 'for as long as you've had a clean licence?'

'Yes,' she replied innocently, 'I have.'

'Then I prefer to take my chances. Tetanus and all,' he added, and before she had time to recover, 'Is this car comprehensively insured?'

She nodded. 'Yes.'

He held out his hand. 'Then give me the keys. I'll drive.'

'You most certainly will not . . .' she began, but for answer, he reached over and picked up her right hand. 'Hold it out,' he said peremptorily. 'Now the left hand. Look well at them.' He allowed her a moment to watch them both trembling like poplar leaves. 'See what I mean? Though I'm not a Nursing Sister, I can tell you you're in no fit state to drive for the moment. Now give me the keys like a sensible girl and get into the passenger seat. I'm late enough as it is.'

He went round and opened the door for her.

With as good a grace as she could muster,

Virginia got herself into the passenger seat. She clasped her hands on her knees and tried to compose her thoughts. Her feelings were quite beyond any possible composition. She was torn by conflicting emotions, as if the stranger had split her normally well balanced personality into two irreconcilable halves. On the one side she was conscious of a burning, choking resentment of this man's tough and arrogant handling of the situation, while on the other side she felt a genuine humble desire to make amends.

When the stranger inserted the key in the ignition of her car, the resentful half of her hoped earnestly that the ancient Ford, always a tricky starter, would go into her frequent act of a groan and a cough and a dying away sigh. Perhaps after several attempts he might give up, and she would have the pleasure of telling him just how much choke and how much accelerator would work the miracle.

The miracle of course happened without her. With a twist of his knowledgeable fingers, the engine fired and caught. His plimsolled foot on the accelerator produced exactly the right amount of pressure. He released the handbrake without its usual graunch and smoothly they slid away.

'I expect you know a lot about engines,' she said, as if to explain the disloyalty of the car to herself, 'working on the airport.'

He nodded modestly, 'A little.'

She watched his big hands on the wheel as he guided her car skilfully into a double lane highway, getting quite a sizeable turn of speed out of her. He was obviously in a hurry to get to his work, she thought, her resentment dying away into concern.

On either side of the road now was a high wire
fence and behind the fences huge cliffs of exciting-
looking buildings, hangars, a skyscraper that
looked as if it was made of mirrors, a heliport. In
one of these, probably, the man worked. Perhaps
he serviced an aircraft like the one momentarily
above them now, its enormous wheels extended.

'Look,' she said when the noise of the aircraft
faded, 'if you'll promise to get that cut seen to some
time today, I suggest I drop you off at your place of
work *before* going to the medical centre.' She consulted her wrist watch. Her hands, she was pleased
to see, were now much steadier, though her heart
was going into all sorts of strange fibrillations.
'I've still got a good fifteen minutes before my
appointment.'

The stranger did not reply. He seemed to be
considering her offer, or perhaps he was simply
concentrating on the now heavy traffic making for
the airport. Now behind the fence were huge aircraft beached like great white whales sporting the
colours of dozens of countries.

Skilfully he insinuated the car between a white
Land Rover with a blipping yellow light and a
bus carrying blue-uniformed men and girls, and
stopped outside the closed metal gate. An airport
policeman raised the gate and waved them in.

'That's all right, thanks,' the stranger replied at
last. 'We're very close now to where I work.' He
swung the car round the open end of a huge hangar
where Virginia glimpsed as in a strange Aladdin's
cave, pieces of silver wing, jewel-coloured lights,
and showers of golden sparks.

'It must be fascinating, your work,' she re-marked.

'It is.' He was busy looking for a place to park. Neatly he backed her car into a vacant slot, pulled on the handbrake and switched off. 'There's where you want, young woman.' He nodded towards a two-storey concrete building with a red cross beside its entrance and the words Entwick Airport Medical Centre in big blue letters. He handed her the keys.

'I'd better give you my name and address,' she said, stiffly opening her handbag. 'Then I can re-imburse you for your bike.'

'Forget it,' he was already getting out of the car, impatient to be off. 'The boys in the hangar will straighten it out in no time.' He walked round to the rear, lifted up the hatchback and hauled out the battered bike, then slammed down the lid.

'Then please,' Virginia fumbled in her hand-bag, found her wallet, and seized a handful of notes. 'Please give them these—the boys in the hangar.'

But clearly she had insulted him. He waved them away, and said frowning, 'Just you mind how you drive on the way home!' Then without a wave or a nod, he turned away and strode towards the hangar.

She watched his tall broad-shouldered figure till it disappeared inside the hangar. He never looked back.

Not that Virginia cared whether he looked back or he didn't. She neither expected nor wanted to see him again. Apart from a purely clinical hope that he had the abrasion professionally dressed, she had no feelings about him at all. She was very sorry about the accident, and angry with herself for missing the white lines. She was not in the slightest put out that the man had not wanted her name and address, that he had no interest whatever in her as a person. He had been generous in not requiring reimbursement. And she was grateful, surely, for that.

What she was not grateful for was the curious body blow that the whole incident had given to her self-esteem, a self-esteem that had only just begun to recover from Peter's defection to a younger woman, a widow apparently, who was much more attractive.

Now, as Virginia waited in the large reception hall of the medical centre, she could feel the last drops of her self-esteem draining away through the soles of her well-polished shoes like unstaunchable life-blood. She was aware, as she unseeingly turned the pages of an airline house magazine, that a pretty and well-groomed blonde receptionist was watching her curiously through the louvred glass of her office window. Perhaps it was part of the receptionist's job, Virginia amused herself by thinking, to size up the nervousness or otherwise of the interviewees as they waited their turn. The previous interviewee had gone in ten minutes after Virginia had arrived, and was still there, though it was now half past four, and a trolley of tea had been wheeled into the interview room.

Perhaps that meant this previous applicant had been successful, and would now be offered the job along with the tea. Perhaps Virginia would shortly be told that she could now go home. Not that she cared, she told herself. Applying for the job had been an impulse, a sudden realisation that now she must strike out, put the past behind her, forget about Peter Willoughby and start afresh.

Not that the past was all painful. She loved her job in Casualty at St Leonard's, and staying near her grandmother had been a self-appointed and loving duty, which she had never found irksome and never regretted. Her parents, whom she could scarcely remember, had died in India, and she had been brought up by her grandmother. Her grandmother's death, like Peter's falling out of love with her, had all happened in the last traumatic six months. Her grandmother had always said that bad things never happened singly, and that was true.

But she was over all that, Virginia told herself. She would find a new job, widen her horizons, try to see something of that great blue globe of the world that stood beside a handsome cheeseplant on the table of the reception hall. On the wall just above the globe was pinned the largest map she had ever seen, with the unnecessary but inviting caption, THE WORLD.

If she was offered the job, and at least her qualifications for it were good, she would be allowed concession fares along the thin red cotton lines that fanned out from the tiny centre that was Entwick across to the four corners of the map —China, New Zealand, Peru, America. A wistful thought came into her mind that a year ago, Peter and she had been planning a honeymoon trip half-way along one of those red routes, but she crushed the thought down.

She checked her wrist watch with the big white face of the clock on the wall, and the receptionist slid open her window to remark cheerfully, 'Shouldn't be long now, Sister. It seems the previous one's been done.'

'I didn't see her go through.' Virginia put the magazine neatly back on the pile, smoothed her short black wavy hair, and tried to put her mind into the correct frame for an interview.

'Oh, you wouldn't,' the girl said. 'There's another exit at the other side of the building, leads along a glass corridor right into the main building. I know she's out, because a light comes on in my office. It's the same if the Chief's doing a medical or a clinic. In a moment there'll be a buzzer and that'll tell me to send you in. So, if you want to comb your hair or dab a bit of powder on, I'd do it now if I were you.'

Virginia had not been wanting to, but it seemed churlish not to. She smiled her thanks, brought out her compact and opened it. She dabbed her nose, but avoided powdering her cheeks, which for some reason looked even paler than usual. From the mirror, her large grey eyes, normally steady and reassuring, looked back at her gravely and with unwonted uncertainty.

She snapped her compact shut. The accident with the cyclist had jangled her nerves, and she almost jumped out of her skin when the buzzer sounded.

'You'll find they're a nice bunch really,' said the receptionist, coming out from behind her window. 'The one in the middle of the three men is the one you've got to please—the Chief Medical Officer, always known as the Chief. The other doctor's a poppet, he won't give you any difficult questions. But it's the Chief that'll decide.'

She preceded Virginia down a short corridor and opened a white-painted door into a bright and sun-filled office.

On the other side of the door stood a man of about forty with sandy hair neatly cut and a pleasant smile. 'I'm Kenneth Milner-Brown,' he said, putting out his hand, 'Administrative Executive Officer at Worldwide's Entwick base. My colleagues and I are sorry to have kept you for so long. Now if you'd be kind enough to sit down.' He waved her to a chair in front of a table, then went behind it, first to adjust the slats of the sunblind, and then to resume his seat beside the other three figures—a broad-shouldered man, an elderly gentleman with white hair and a pointed beard, and a plump woman—all silhouetted against the ribs of sunlight.

Seeing Virginia blink, Mr Milner-Brown leapt to his feet and again adjusted the blind. She smiled her thanks and studied the four members of the selection board. Unlike Mr Milner-Brown, who was dressed in a neat fawn suit, the other two men wore white doctors' coats and the middle-aged woman was in the uniform of a Senior Nursing Sister.

As she perched on the edge of her chair, Virginia was distantly aware that the Nursing Sister had leaned forward to offer her some tea, but she heard herself declining it, because she knew her hands would begin to tremble again. For she now realised to her dismay that she was still in a state of shock.

She blinked her eyes in alarm and tried to take a very firm grip on herself. The effect of the accident must have been greater than she had supposed —frequently shock did not immediately manifest itself—but now it was impairing her vision and causing her to hallucinate.

She looked at the face of the man opposite her, the man sitting in the middle of the three men, the man the receptionist had said would decide, trying desperately to clear her brain. But the hallucination persisted. She kept seeing the face of the blue-jeaned cyclist superimposed above the white lapels of the doctor's coat.

She curled her toes inside her neat court shoes, hoping to lower her blood pressure, then stole another look at him. Eyes of the same vivid intense blue as the cyclist's met hers. A polite smile curved the firm sculpted lips. 'And now may I introduce the other three of the quorum,' the man said slowly in that deep rich unforgettable voice, 'Our invaluable Sister Monica Porter, who is our most senior Sister.' The Senior Nursing Sister smiled, her chubby cheeks dimpled with pleasure. He smiled towards the white-haired bearded doctor. 'Dr Marcus Lascelles, who is a walking encyclopedeia on aviation medicine. And myself,' his big mechanic's hands touched the plastic identity tag on his white coat, 'Richard Tranter, Chief Medical Officer.'

Even at that late stage, Virginia tried to convince herself that he was not the *actual* blue-jeaned cyclist, that this Chief Medical Officer was simply the cyclist's double or his twin brother.

But suddenly the Chief bent his head to study her

documents on the table in front of him, and unmistakably now, she could see on his forehead, immediately beneath the line of his dark red hair, a piece of sticking plaster hastily applied.

'Shall we begin?' he asked urbanely as she sat staring as if hypnotised by that piece of plaster. He turned to the other two. 'I should tell you that Sister Mayhew and I met earlier today.' He paused for an excessively long time. *'Quite by accident.'*

Those three words so satirically uttered had a healthy astringent effect on Virginia. Indignation against this supercilious doctor, who by not disclosing his identity earlier had allowed her to make a fool of herself, sent a plentiful supply of adrenalin pumping through her veins. Her eyes sparkled, her cheeks flushed, her back stiffened, the flowing away of her self-esteem was staunched. She answered Dr Tranter's questions clearly and concisely. He asked her about her training at the West London Hospital, about her first job in Fulham, her experience in the operating theatre and later in Casualty. He asked her if she knew anything about the effects of flying, and the most common complaints suffered by passengers.

'I have no direct experience,' she answered truthfully. 'But I can hazard a guess that baratrauma would be one of them—oedema, difficulties because of alteration to the Circadian rhythm, and collapse due to tension and fear of flying. But it's something I would have to learn more about.'

He gave her a nod. It seemed to be the right answer.

Only once did the adrenalin fail her. He asked

her if she had watched the great Professor Gaunt operate.

She paused. Peter had been the great Professor's Registrar, at one stage his blue-eyed boy. They had met at one of the Professor's famous parties.

With an effort, she answered coolly, 'Yes, several times.'

And then, having negotiated that hurdle, Dr Tranter asked with deceptive mildness, 'Is there any pressing personal reason why you wish to change the lights of London for an airport in the country?'

Dismissing the idea that he was such a good diagnostician that he could put his finger intuitively on a half-healed wound, Virginia answered politely, 'I have several personal reasons, Dr Tranter, but none of them pressing.'

A little quirk of cynical amusement twitched his mouth as if he could see far beyond *that* answer. But he made no comment.

With a wave of his hand, a deepening of the quirky smile, he turned to the bearded doctor. 'Your witness, Mark,' he said lightly, and sat back, arms folded across his chest, to fix an unblinking gaze on Virginia's face.

'You mentioned interruption to the Circadian rhythm,' said Dr Lascelles, stroking his beard, 'I wonder if you know if people suffer from it more travelling east to west than they do travelling north to south?'

'Yes,' she answered promptly, 'they do. Because travelling east/west they're crossing time zones, and this upsets their body rhythm.'

'Excellent, excellent,' Dr Lascelles smiled. 'I

have no more questions. Sister Porter?'

The Senior Nursing Sister's questions were routine and easy. She asked about Virginia's knowledge of the new techniques on third-degree burns, her experience of ophthalmic surgery and skill allergies, especially industrial allergies.

'What we explain to all the candidates is this,' Sister Porter went on. 'We supply medical cover for everyone on the airport, while they're on the airport.' She smiled expectantly at Virginia.

'Quite an undertaking—especially at peak times.'

'Indeed it is. An airport at peak time is a busy town in itself. And besides all those passengers, we have the aircrew, the ground staff, ancillary workers, personnel from construction firms, and catering firms,' Sister Porter held up her hand and counted them off on her plump well-manicured fingers. 'As well as that, our section gives the pilots their very stringent six-monthly medicals. We're a small team and a busy one,' she threw a sideways admiring smile at the Chief, 'but a very happy one.'

Virginia did not dare to follow the direction of the Senior Sister's smile. She knew that the Chief's eyes were fixed on her own face, and she found them difficult to meet.

'We work straightforward shifts,' Sister Porter went on. 'There's rarely a slack moment. At a second's notice we can be faced with an emergency, so we're always on our toes.'

Having delivered herself of that, the Senior Sister sat back in her chair, but first, Virginia noticed she looked for a nod of approval from her Chief, and having received it, went pink with pleasure.

The girl in Reception seemed to have been right; the Chief, the man sitting in the middle, was going to decide.

With a wave of his large hand, the Chief now indicated that Mr Milner-Brown should question her. He gave her his reassuring smile and asked her what had attracted her to working at an airport. It was not a difficult question to answer. In any case, Mr Milner-Brown was so entranced with the subject himself that he did most of the answering. Enthusiastically he finished up, 'It's like the map we have hanging in the reception hall, the whole world comes to your doorstep.'

'The whole world and its *ills*,' Dr Tranter said drily.

'Ah, yes,' the Executive Officer agreed. 'But what a challenge!'

He seemed to have no more questions to put to Virginia. She was asked by Dr Tranter if she had any questions to ask of them, and in no time she was being asked to wait in a small ante-room by the back entrance.

The walls were thin and she could hear the murmur of voices as her candidacy was discussed. She tried not to listen, but Dr Tranter's voice had a penetrating quality that seemed pitched to her reluctant ear. She heard him say decisively, 'She's what we need—highly qualified, not too young, and not too attractive.'

Two minutes later, when she was recalled to be offered the job, all she could think of was that she wished she had the strength of mind to turn it down.

CHAPTER TWO

FOR the next hour she continued to regret it. Once they had all shaken her by the hand, Dr Tranter pushed back his chair and brought the meeting back to earth by reminding her, 'Of course you understand the offer is dependent on your passing the medical.'

Virginia nodded. 'Yes, I understand.' She cleared her throat and asked, 'And when do I come for that?'

Dr Tranter consulted his wrist watch, closed his eyes as if making some mental calculations and opened them again. 'There's no time like the present. If we get a move on, I can just fit you in now. I'll send her round to you after that, Ken, and you can fill in all your bumph,' then nodding dismissingly to the bearded doctor and Mr Milner-Brown and the Nursing Sister, 'Many thanks to you three for your invaluable help.'

He stood up, walked towards the door and beckoned for Virginia to follow him. 'No need to be nervous,' he threw at her over his shoulder. 'You look healthy enough to me. You should be all right.'

'I'm not nervous,' she replied.

The doctor's white-coated shoulders managed to express disbelief as he preceded her down the corridor through the reception hall to another white-painted door marked Aircrew Medical

Examination Centre. 'Don't be put off by that,' Dr
Tranter said, smiling as he opened the door.
'You're not going to get the full aircrew medical.
Though I shall put the ruler over you pretty
thoroughly—because if there's one thing we can't
do with here, it's a sick nurse.'

Virginia gritted her teeth and said nothing.

'You can undress there, behind that curtain.
Down to your pants. Come out when you're ready.
Try not to be too long.'

She heard him whistling tunelessly to himself as
she undressed and slipped into the white operating
gown that had been hanging on a hook.

'Good,' he said as she emerged. 'At least you did
that quickly.' He brought out his stethoscope,
warmed it thoughtfully for a moment in his fingers
and placed it against her chest. He listened gravely.
'Are you sure you're not nervous?' he asked, listening thoughtfully.

'I might be just a little.'

'Ah,' he seemed to find the admission amusing,
'otherwise I would have said your heart rate was
somewhat high.'

'Today has been very exciting,' she said
apologetically.

He shot her an amused superior smile but made
no comment.

Satisfied on heart and lungs, he took her blood
pressure, looked down her throat and into her ears
and eyes, tested her reflexes and her vision. He
put her on the scales and clicked his tongue disapprovingly and said, 'My goodness, you are a
lightweight!'

Then she lay on the couch while he palpated her

spleen and liver. To her dismay she felt as embarrassed as a young girl.

With relief that it was soon to be over, she heard him say, 'Now you can sit down,' he indicated a chair beside his desk, 'and help me fill in one of these damned forms. Then I'll send you through to X-Ray for a couple of candid camera shots of you, and then we'll be finished.'

Virginia subsided into the metal chair and clutched her robe round herself. Outside aircraft engines roared, she heard the thunder of a heavy tractor, the whine of metal on metal from the hangars. But the examination room seemed contained in its own oddly intimate and intimidating quiet, as if everything they did was momentous.

She watched him draw out a long form from the drawer, lay it on his desk, smooth it carefully and unscrew his pen.

'Right, are you ready? Then I'll fire away.'

He asked her about her parents and where she was born, her childish ailments, any allergies she might have, any operations, any serious illnesses whether she smoked or drank, or had ever taken drugs, and in the same unemotional tone as if he'd heard it all before, 'And I presume you're coming down here to forget some man?'

'No,' she said, flushing scarlet.

'I thought I was right.' He put a final tick beside some box on the medical form, signed it and looked up at her.

'OK.' He pressed a buzzer on the side of his desk. 'I'll hand you over now to our radiographer Clare Todd.' As he spoke that name his expression subtly changed, became less remote, almost vulnerable.

Then he looked at his watch and whistled as if Sister Mayhew had taken up far more than her allotted time. 'Thank you, Sister. I'll say goodbye. Take your clothes with you into X-Ray, then you don't need to come back.' He stood up. 'Oh, by the way, I've had a report from the hangar, and the prognosis on the bike is good.'

He waved Virginia towards a communicating door that had just opened. Framed in it stood a slender woman of about twenty-seven, her bright auburn hair vivid against her starched white coat. From under beautifully arched eyebrows, green eyes regarded Virginia suspiciously and assessingly.

'The usual, Clare,' said Dr Tranter, not bothering to introduce them. 'Then point her in the direction of Ken Milner-Brown. I must be on my way. See you this evening.'

'Eightish,' Clare smiled brilliantly.

'I'll be on the dot.'

Simple words, but something warm and tender in their tone made them eminently revealing ones. Virginia thought, with a little catch in her throat, Clare Todd and the impossible Dr Tranter were in love.

They were well matched, Virginia decided by the time she left the X-ray department. Both were efficient, both high-handed, both interested in their jobs, both clear it seemed in what they wanted out of life.

Virginia had found herself observing the radiographer closely, an observation which was mutual. The bright green eyes seemed to miss nothing, while in turn, Virginia's eyes saw almost immediately, as the radiographer slid the first plate into the X-ray machine, that there was a pink band round the third finger of her left hand as if when not X-raying, she wore a wedding or engagement ring.

That the radiographer was of outstanding attractiveness required no acute observation. She had the fine creamy skin that looks especially radiant with auburn hair. Her brows and lashes were as black as Sister Mayhew's. Her teeth were even and perfect, her lips full and sensuous.

She walked with the sinuous movement of someone who knows how shapely is her figure as she disappeared into the darkroom to check the wets. 'They're fine,' she said, coming back wiping her fingers on a towel. She looked Virginia over again with barely shielded curiosity. 'Think you'll settle down here all right?'

'I sincerely hope so.'

'It's very hard work.'

'I'm used to hard work.'

'It's very cliquey, if you know what I mean. You're either an in-person or you're not.'

Her narrowed eyes and her acid smiled indicated that she had no doubt into which category Sister Mayhew would fall. Not waiting to see if she was offered any instructions on how to get to the administrative section, Virginia dressed and made her escape.

In any case, the receptionist was informative. 'Go down that corridor to your left. It leads to the back of our medical building and the glass corridor that connects us to the main terminal. You'll use that corridor a lot when you come here. The Chief calls it the Glass Cord.' Then she added, smiling, 'I'm ever so glad you got the job.'

'Thank you very much.' Virginia smiled and flushed with pleasure.

'Yes,' the girl said, 'I bet myself you would.'

'Oh?'

'I always do. It's like picking a horse. My name's Rosie Smith, but there's a lot of Irish in me. My mother was Irish. Of course you can't put money on it or anything, but it makes it more interesting.'

'I'm sure it does, and I think it was very clever of you.'

'Not really. I knew what they were looking for.' Rosie took a deep breath as if she was about to go on, and then thought better of it. Virginia did not embarrass the girl by telling her that she too knew what they were looking for—someone efficient, experienced and not too attractive.

Instead, she hitched her bag on to her shoulder and left for the more soothing ministrations of Mr Milner-Brown.

'You're exactly the person we were looking for,' he said, translating the Chief Medical Officer's comments into a far sweeter one. 'A Nursing Sister of splendid qualifications and outstanding character, as your references have told us. And as we could see for ourselves, of a pleasing personality, but not a flibberty-gibbet.'

He then sat her down at a table where she filled in more forms, sipped the cup of tea which he placed at her elbow and finally left clutching a list of recommended accommodation.

Half an hour later she was knocking on the door of the first on the list, No. 7 The Ridgeway, a semi-detached brick and tile-hung house on the outskirts of a village about three miles from the airport. The front garden was a skilfully controlled riot of roses and geraniums. A male voice answered in reply to her knock, 'The door is open, and you're late.'

She knocked again, and the male voice answered exasperatedly, 'Turn the handle, for heaven's sake! I'm busy painting the window frame!'

Feeling like Goldilocks, Virginia turned the handle and went inside.

The door opened almost straight into a very well furnished lounge that went through to french windows at the back. Father Bear, a brown-haired chubby man in his late thirties, was standing by the window. He wore an old fawn sweater, and held a paint pot in his hand. He looked up, began to say, 'I've . . .' then demanded, 'Who are you? You're not my wife. I was expecting my wife—I thought she'd forgotten her key. Who are you?'

Virginia had scarcely told him her name and her errand, when the front door was flung open, and this time, laden with parcels, in rustled his wife. A few years his junior, she too was inclined to plumpness. But her brown hair was stylishly cut, freshly washed and gleaming. Her pretty round face was carefully made up and her lovely bright eyes were restless. Her smile was unaffectedly welcoming, as if Virginia's advent was exactly the diversion she had been hoping for.

'I'd heard,' she said as she divested herself of her numerous parcels, 'that they were interviewing for your job today. Ken Milner-Brown said someone might come along, but I didn't expect you quite so soon. It *is* about the bed-sitter you've come, isn't it? Well then, let me show you it!'

She swept Virginia off upstairs, chattering as she went.

The house had three nice-sized bedrooms, she said, and two tiny bathrooms, so Sister Mayhew could therefore have her own. She led her into the second best bedroom. It was covered in a thick mushroom carpet. There was a large window that looked towards the airport, and through it, Virginia could see the huge head of the radar still sweeping backwards and forwards on its endless scan.

'That's just been installed, that new radar bowl,' said Mrs Best, following her gaze. 'One of the biggest in Europe.'

'I can quite believe it.' Virginia continued to look at it reproachfully. Perhaps it would be no bad thing to see it every morning when she parted the pretty frilly curtains, to remind her to give Dr Tranter as wide as possible a berth.

'Plenty of cupboards,' Mrs Best said, drawing her attention to the furnishings. 'And that makes into a desk-cum-dressing table. We both work. We've been married for over six years. We've no children, so we've been able to fix the house up quite well.'

'Does your husband work at the airport?'

'Close by. He's got a very unglamorous job really—he's a quality controller at Sugdens. But I've got a very glamorous one—at least, *I* think it is. I'm a professional aunt, for the airline.'

'A professional airline aunt? I didn't even know they existed.'

'Well, you do now,' Mrs Best beamed as if explaining about airline aunts was one of her favourite topics. 'They've been going for some time over at Gatwick, and now we've started airline aunts here. We can be called out at a moment's notice to travel with unaccompanied children to any place our airline flies to.'

'It sounds wonderful,' smiled Virginia.

'Oh, it is!'

'And very worthwhile.'

'*I* think so. We take good care of them, give them a bit of mothering. Because partings are always sad, aren't they?'

'Yes,' Virginia said softly, 'very sad.'

'When I meet my brood and see them wearing our discs, I want to get my arms round each and every one. I've got a disc on me—I'll show you what I mean.' Mrs Best dipped her hand into her jacket pocket and brought out a white disc, edged with the red and blue of the airline colours, upon which was printed simply and sadly UNACCOMPANIED. PLEASE HELP.

'I sometimes think,' Mrs Best smiled wryly, 'that we could all do with a disc like that.'

Virginia nodded wistfully.

'Mind, they're only a precaution, in case a child got separated, which we make sure they don't.'

'And how often do you go on these trips?'

'Not so often as I'd like.' Mrs Best's light brown eyes sparkled. 'It's a marvellous way to get out of the rut.'

'And you like children, obviously.'

'Oh, yes. We intend to have our own some day, but not yet. Anyway, enough about me. Have a good look round the room, see what you think. Try the bed—it's very comfortable.'

Mrs Best sat down on the edge of the divan and bounced up and down to demonstrate the springs. She waved for Virginia to do the same. 'The terms of the room with bathroom, breakfast and evening meal . . .' she named a very reasonable sum. 'Will you take it?'

'Yes, thank you, I'd like to. Though I think it's worth more.'

Then to Virginia's astonishment, instead of smiling, Mrs Best covered her face with her hands and burst into tears. 'Oh, I'm so glad,' she whispered hoarsely, as the tears squeezed through her fingers. 'So thankful! You've no idea how awful it's been these last few weeks. You see, I've suddenly realised my husband doesn't love me any more, and it's such a relief to have someone to talk to about it.'

As she patted Mrs Best's shoulder comfortingly, Virginia felt a sad sense of inevitability and an almost sisterly empathy with Mrs Best as she remembered again her own sense of abandonment and loss.

Dr Tranter had been right: she had come here to forget a man. Now she knew she couldn't forget.

CHAPTER THREE

Six weeks later, when Virginia set out for her first day's duty at the medical section of Entwick Airport, wearing her brand-new uniform, she carried with her something that was calculated to make her forget. It was a cutting from the *Daily Telegraph* announcing the forthcoming marriage of Dr Peter Willoughby and Mrs Antonia Villiers. The marriage was to take place in two weeks' time. The cutting had been sent for kind and therapeutic purposes by a former colleague at St Leonard's, and though it stung like iodine in an open wound, Virginia resolved to carry it, if not close to her heart, at least close to her person.

She also carried with her, though in her head and not in print, a list of dos and don'ts from Beryl Best, given to her over her first breakfast along with a fresh boiled egg and home-made bread. Beryl, like all good aunts, kept her ear to the ground and knew what was going on.

'Do keep Clare Todd in her place, dear. She thinks because she's got the Chief in tow, she can do what she likes. And on the subject of the Chief, don't let him ride roughshod over you.'

The list had continued with who could tell who what to do, and who couldn't, who could use which dining room and what parking place, who could be trusted implicitly, who on occasions and who not at all, moving back, naturally it seemed, to Clare

Todd and Dr Tranter. 'She's in the last category.
Don't trust her at all—not personally. You can
trust her work, apparently. That's very good, they
say. Dr Tranter certainly thinks so, but he would.
And on the subject of him again, do remember he's
a slavedriver. Never leaves the centre. A workaholic. Though . . .' a sad thought had struck her,
'all these years, I've thought my Frank, my faithful
Frank, was a workaholic, and now I know it's
someone else. Another woman.'

Virginia had moved in to Number 7 the evening
before. It was the first time Beryl had referred to
their marriage or to her tearful confession that
Frank no longer loved her. Virginia had seen
nothing at all of Frank. She had met him only
briefly when she had arrived and he had left early
for work that morning.

'Perhaps you're wrong now, and it is just work
that keeps him out so much,' Virginia suggested
gently.

Beryl had shaken her head vehemently, pursed
her lips and waved a hand in front of her face to
indicate that she didn't want to talk about Frank
now.

'Is Dr Tranter married?' Virginia asked, recog-
nising that Beryl probably found it therapeutic to
talk about other people and their doings.

Beryl brightened. 'No, not as yet. The sixty-four-
dollar question is *yet*.'

'He's engaged?'

'Not exactly, but near as dammit. He's waiting
for the lady in question, in other words, Clare
Todd, to be free. And thereby hangs a tale.'

'I expect it's too long to tell now.' Virginia

drained her coffee cup in a gesture of finality, and pushed back her chair. Suddenly she didn't want to hear about Dr Tranter and his affairs. She could not explain why, for she had conceived no liking whatsoever for the man, quite the reverse in fact. But the idea of him waiting for Clare Todd to be free spoiled her own personal and private image of Dr Tranter. Though what her image of him was she couldn't define, except that somewhere a steely integrity came into it.

In fact, Virginia thought, driving with consummate care to the airport, that was the quality that had seemed to make her new boss bearable. She frowned severely at the giant head of the radar bowl, as she passed it dementedly swinging above the hedge. High-handed, arrogant and impatient, at least he ought not to have been like Peter and other men.

But he was.

She refused to allow herself to speculate on what the story might be of his affair with Clare Todd. She would no doubt be told soon enough. Meanwhile, she concentrated on her driving. She refused to allow her eyes to be diverted by the aircraft flying low above her. She steered carefully in through the gate, smiling her good morning to the policeman who raised it, trying not to remember that last time she had been sitting beside Dr Tranter, blissfully unaware who he was. Now she found herself a parking place in front of the medical section and backed the car into position. She sat for a moment, drawing in the strange smell of an airport, the mixture of that old-fashioned paraffin of the jets mixing with petrol and dope and dusty concrete.

She glanced nervously up at the façade of the squat building as she locked up, and noticed a familiar bicycle in some concrete slots beside the main entrance. It had acquired a new pair of handlebars, but there were still some battle scars on the frame. Beside Dr Tranter's bicycle was a new glossy female one.

'I bet you don't know whose bicycle that is. I saw you looking enviously at it,' Rosie called out from her glass box in the same breath as she added, 'Good morning, Sister, and welcome.'

Virginia had a very good idea whose bicycle it was, but she wasn't going to cheat Rosie of her fun.

'Yours?' she asked.

'No, not on your life, Sister! I live six miles away, and I get a bus, even though the Chief's on at us to walk or bike.'

'Whose is it, then?' Virginia smilingly played Rosie's little game.

'Our Miss Todd—Clare. Everyone said she'd be the last to get the habit. Normally she drives a white convertible, but I bet myself she would, and I won.'

'Very clever of you,' said Virginia, cross with herself that the information should increase her sense of disappointment.

'Oh, I don't miss much,' Rosie came from behind her glass barrier, and smiling said, 'And now I know you're dying to see your new office. You take over from Senior Sister Porter. She's on nights. Dr Tranter said you'd be working the eight till four for the first three months, under his eagle eye!'

'Yes.'

'Not that it ever does work out eight till four,' added Rosie. 'Eight till evermore, your prede-

cessor used to say. She left to get married—
quite a whirlwind affair. That's why they didn't
want . . . well, anyone who wouldn't stay too long.
Shall I lead the way?'

'Please do.' Virginia followed Rosie across the
reception hall and down a small corridor. The
building was much bigger inside than she had first
supposed, with small corridors fanning out from
the central hall rather like the routes on the airline
map.

'You'll have your name on the door in a moment,
just a card in that slot. We change it with each shift.
It's all part of the airline security, naming everyone. But it's nice, don't you think? Makes you feel
really here.'

At that moment, the door opened from the other
side, and Virginia found herself looking into the
jolly smiling face of Sister Porter, who had been on
her selection board. 'Good morning, Sister
Mayhew, and welcome.' She looked scrubbed and
pink as if she had just come from under a warm
shower instead of night duty. She waved Virginia
into a rectangular office. It had a large window
facing the hangar with a view of the airfield beyond.
'Double-glazed and soundproofed, thank goodness,' Sister Porter said. 'It's always nice and quiet
in here.'

'It's very pleasant,' Virginia smiled, gazing
around at the painted panelled walls, the polished
floor, the comfortable armchairs. A small curtained area hid an examination couch. There was a
red telephone on the wall beside it, some oxygen
cylinders and a resuscitation kit.

'You'll find those items in all the medical rooms

—red override emergency telephone, oxygen and resuscitation kit. But our main equipment is in the treatment room next door. The Chief says he'll take you in hand today and explain what has to be explained.'

Sister Porter walked over to the white-painted tidy desk, empty except for a large open log book. 'Handing over procedure isn't as in a hospital. We don't have report time. Everything is in here.' She pointed to the log book. 'Every case we're called out to, every patient that comes here, is logged —diagnosis, treatment, disposal. As you can see, we weren't madly busy. The day shift, this shift, is the crackingly hard one. The Chief wanted you thrown in at the deep end. Well,' she looked at her watch and unhooked her cape from behind the door, 'I have a hubby about to pick me up—one of the joys of both being on nights!' She patted Virginia's arm in a motherly way. 'Good luck, my dear. Anything you don't know, just ask.' She bustled past Rosie still hovering on the threshold. 'Rosie here is a mine of information. And you'll find the Chief very approachable.'

Scarcely had Sister Porter vanished towards the entrance than there was the sudden flashing of a red light in a three-lamp combination over the door. Simultaneously a buzzer sounded on the desk. Rosie laughed. 'That's himself—the Chief. The flashing red light is always himself. Means he wants you in his office five minutes ago.'

She began to divest Virgina of her cloak. 'His office is through that door—no, not the one we came by, the one behind you. That opens on to the treatment room, and the Chief's office is on the other side of that, next to the room where you had your medical.'

Adjusting her new starched cap with the frivolous pleated edging, and glancing at her wrist watch, Virginia saw it was still ten minutes short of eight o'clock.

'The Chief gets in about seven-thirty, sometimes earlier,' Rosie told her, 'and he's still here when Night Sister takes over. Rumour has it that he never does go home. We have emergency beds ready made up. Miss Todd was in early today too, they cycled in together.'

Virginia said nothing. She drew in a deep breath, crossed the well appointed treatment room and knocked on Dr Tranter's door.

'Come in, Sister.' With a little nervous twist of mingled excitement and apprehension, she heard the deep well-remembered drawl.

Dr Tranter was standing by his window, which looked on to the front entrance and the car park. He had probably watched her arrive, and with a little rebellious thought, she wondered if she had parked the car to his satisfaction.

He turned as she came in and smiled his curiously attractive smile. He took his hands out of the pockets of his white coat and extended his right hand in welcome.

'Good morning, Sister.' She remembered his handshake as she remembered his voice. It was firm and businesslike. 'Welcome aboard. I'm glad you arrived safely.' He paused, then his smile deepened and he raised one eyebrow. 'Without incident, I hope?'

'Without incident,' she repeated cautiously, not

sure if he was teasing her about their previous encounter. 'I hope you did the same?'

'Without any incident worth remembering,' he replied, and waved her to a chair in front of his desk. She found herself looking to see if there were any photographs on the desk, but it was tidy and uncluttered. Dr Tranter's back was to the window. Virginia couldn't read his expression, but she was aware that he was studying her carefully.

'Well now,' he said in a brisk tone, 'you've met Sister Porter again this morning, I take it?'

'Yes, I have.'

'She's our lynch-pin, very experienced. Been here since Entwick was a racecourse—a real stalwart. So is Sister Mortimer. You'll soon get to feel at home.'

'I'm sure I shall,' Virginia agreed.

'We're not nearly so formidable when you get to know us.'

Virginia smiled.

'And you left St Leonard's without too many tears, I hope?'

A glint, not altogether of humour, sparkled in his blue eyes. He seemed to be half teasing, half probing—still no doubt believing she had left London to forget some man.

'I was sorry to leave in many ways,' she answered.

'Disposed of your flat all right, did you?'

'It was only a bed-sitter, so I'd no difficulty. In fact, I had a queue.'

'And you've settled in where?'

'With the Bests at Number 7, The Ridgeway.'

'Ah, yes, I know—the escort aunt. Nice girl.

Nice couple, in fact. Trouble is she suffers from itchy feet. By that I mean the desire to travel, not anything in the clinical sense.'

'I realised that.'

'Good. Well, Mrs Best no doubt filled you in with the airline gossip.'

'She filled me in with something of the background,' Virginia corrected.

Dr Tranter shot her a disbelieving smile. 'As you wish. It boils down, no doubt, to the same thing.' He opened the top drawer of his desk and drew out a form. 'And you intend to drive that old rattletrap in every day, do you?'

'I intend, Doctor, to drive my estate car in every day. And it's in excellent running order. It had no difficulty passing its MOT.'

He held up his large well-shaped hand. 'Don't get so defensive! And don't waste your maternal instincts on a car,' he said lightly and with a smile, but Virginia felt her cheeks flush with anger. 'What's the number?'

'TAP 456,' she reeled off promptly.

'We need that for security,' he explained, writing the number down on a form. 'An airport has to be very security-conscious, as you'll discover. And it's especially security-conscious for people such as ourselves who must have immediate admittance to all zones of security, even the sensitive Airside zone. And it's very watchful of any cars left parked, so you have to have a permit.' At that point his voice changed from being crisply informative to that of someone mounting his special hobbyhorse. 'Of course, it's much better for your health to cycle to work.' He paused and added with wry emphasis,

'And much better for other people's health, I shouldn't wonder.' He fingered the small scar on his forehead meaningfully.

Virginia flushed. She felt herself thrown into a state of emotional confusion. This doctor sitting so laconically opposite her, so much the master of the situation, was like no one she had ever met before. She couldn't size him up. She felt such a variety of contradictory reactions to his presence that it was as if she had lost her foothold on her normally well-controlled world.

He made her feel excited and stimulated as if she really were starting a new life. He made her feel reassured on the one hand by his masculinity and, on the other, threatened and angered by what could turn into dominance. She was not sure how to react to him, when he was teasing her and when he wasn't. Certainly he had little deep cut lines beside his mouth as if he often smiled that quirky humorous smile, but the mouth itself, straight and well-shaped, had a way of setting into quite forbidding severity.

But worse than all these facets of his complicated character was a way he had, totally unconscious of course, of making her feel terribly aware of him and concerned for him. Now she felt an immediate concern for that wretched little scar on his forehead which her professional self tried to tell her was very cleanly healed and of no consequence whatsoever.

'Did it take long to heal?' she heard herself ask. 'The contusion?'

'This?' The quirky lines deepened. 'Of course not.'

'I hope,' she went on earnestly, 'that you haven't suffered any ill-effects. Any headaches?'

'Not *headaches*,' he replied cryptically, leaving her with the lingering suspicion that he might have suffered other unnamed ill-effects. Then he looked up suddenly and laughed at her troubled expression. 'Don't look so conscience-stricken, Sister! I was only teasing you. Did you never have any brothers who teased you?'

'No,' she said flatly. For some reason the idea of a brotherly teasing depressed her when really she should have felt flattered.

'Pity,' he sighed. 'Because I do believe that behind that cool efficient self-contained exterior there lurks . . .' But he stopped himself saying what he believed lurked.

He cleared his throat as if recalling himself to business, and looked down again at his desk. 'So you'll need a security clearance and docket for your *estate car.*' He emphasised the last two words with a little inward-turning smile. 'And you yourself will be issued with an ID card—red zone, which means admission anywhere. You'll need a bleeper, similar to a hospital bleeper. And this little device.' He tilted his chair over and reached out a long arm to unhook a small rectangular object like a pocket calculator. 'This is a special radio key known as a token which will unlock any door. You wear it on your belt. Leaves both your hands free. Wear it when you get a call to any Airside building. When not in use it has to be clipped to its wall holder to recharge.' He leaned over to replace it. 'So.'

Virginia was just thinking rather mistily that it was a pity there wasn't a device that would unlock people and deciding perhaps it wouldn't be a good thing if there was, when she realised Dr Tranter was talking to her again.

'We'll set all this in motion, if you'll now give me the passport photos you were told to bring with you.'

Perhaps he expected, Virginia thought uncharitably, that she might have forgotten to bring them and that he would have an opportunity to further reprove her.

'Yes, of course.' She gave him a confident smile, opened her handbag, took out her wallet and withdrew the passport photographs. Unfortunately, as she drew out the photographs, out too came the folded cutting from the *Daily Telegraph*. Like a paper dart, it went skimming across the polished desk and on to Dr Tranter's lap.

He picked it up, seemed about to hand it back to her, then appeared to have second and more evil thoughts. Perhaps it was her indrawn breath, and the widening of her eyes. Perhaps it was merely the contentiousness and high-handedness of his own nature that caused him to hold the piece of paper fastidiously aloft in his long fingers and shoot her a penetrating diagnostic glance.

'Something important, is it, Sister?' she heard him ask coldly.

'No, it's nothing. Nothing important whatsoever.'

'Something personal, perhaps?'

'Certainly not!'

'Then,' he raised an eyebow, 'you won't mind if I look at it?'

Taking her silence for consent, he unfolded it, then read it, first to himself and then, unforgivably, *aloud*.

By the time he had finished reading, any lingering liking Virginia had had for Dr Tranter had vanished, and she felt as outraged as if he had physically struck her.

'Peter Willoughby,' he said musingly and derisively. 'So that's who it is—Peter Willoughby! The chap running the smart new Kensington Clinic.' He clicked his tongue. 'Fancy that!'

Virginia's large grey eyes blazed, but she said nothing.

'Still in love with him, are you?' Dr Tranter threw her another of those keen diagnostic glances.

'No.'

'Sure?'

'Quite sure.'

'Well, thank your lucky stars for that.' He paused and went on quietly, 'He's not worth a single tear, believe you me.'

'I don't believe you!' The words were wrung out of her angrily and vehemently and in anguish. She never intended to say them; she intended to hold her tongue and her peace.

'You will,' Dr Tranter told her quietly, 'one of these days.' He seemed suddenly to become aware that he was still holding the cutting. He looked down at it with an expression of dislike and contempt. 'Meantime, you won't need this, I promise you.' And to her horror, slowly and deliberately he tore the cutting in half and then in quarters, got to his feet and threw the pieces in the wastepaper basket. In a quite different tone of voice he went on sternly, 'As far as you're concerned, the past is over—remember that. This is an important medical centre. We don't run a cure here for the lovelorn.'

CHAPTER FOUR

'But it seems we run a cure for everything else,' Dr Tranter remarked to Virginia that afternoon. The tone of his voice was light, as if he were reminding her of his warning and at the same time taking the sting out of his own harsh words.

Virginia nodded, but said nothing. She was sitting at her desk with the big medical incident ledger open in front of her. Under Dr Tranter's supervision, she was entering their latest treatment, a young workman who had fallen off the scaffolding on the heliport and sustained a fractured femur and who was now on his way to the County Hospital. He was the twentieth of a daunting variety of emergencies which they had dealt with that day. Time had sped by, and there had been no time to eat any lunch. Dr Tranter and she had worked well together. She had forgotten her anger and anguish of earlier this morning, and totally forgotten about Peter.

Until now.

Now Dr Tranter was forcing her to remember both. 'This,' he said, leaning over her shoulder, and pointing so that the sleeve of his white coat brushed her cheek, 'this,' he emphasised, his finger tip travelling down the entries, 'is why you can't afford to have your mind on anything but the job.' He read out (he seemed fond, Virginia thought, of reading aloud) their diagnoses and treatments for

46

the day. The coronary, happily not severe, which had begun their day, the two epileptic fits, the diabetic passenger brought off the aircraft in a coma, an acute appendicitis, the child who had swallowed a coin, the elderly woman who had fallen down the stairs, the incoming flight from Cairo carrying passengers with suspected food poisoning . . . the list was too long even for Dr Tranter to read aloud.

'And all these patients were people you'd never seen in your life before, weren't they?'

'Yes.'

'It'll always be like that—or almost always. The staff patients you may have seen before, but almost never the passengers. You haven't case notes like you have in hospital. Often you don't even speak their language. Sometimes they're unconscious or too ill to tell you anything. Do you see what I mean?'

'I always did, Doctor.' Virginia replied stiffly and even to her own ears rather resentfully.

Dr Tranter sighed. Brusquely, he said, pointing to the screw-top thermos flask on her desk, 'I should have a drink of coffee now while you've got the chance. Clare will no doubt have left some sandwiches for us in the Night Sister's kitchen.'

He turned round and she heard him striding along to the kitchen. He returned a moment later with the pleased endearing smile of a schoolboy, bearing an open plastic box. 'Smoked salmon,' he said. 'My favourite. Clare's very thoughtful.' He held out the box to Virginia. 'Grab a handful. Hunger can make people irritable.'

Virginia frowned. She was sure the sandwiches

would have choked her, but she was spared the trouble of finding out. The telephone on her desk shrilled, and the two red lights flashed above the door. Dr Tranter leaned across and answered the telephone before her.

'Medical Section,' he announced. 'Yes, Tranter speaking. Go ahead.' He listened carefully, his dark brows drawn together. 'Any pain?' He listened again. 'Mm. But you think it's a coronary?' He listened again, then he asked, 'Who's with her at the moment? I see, in the Customs Hall. OK, we'll be right down.'

Even before he had replaced the receiver, Virginia had unhooked the mobile resuscitation kit and clipped on to her belt the radio key.

'Suspected coronary,' Dr Tranter told her. 'Main Customs Hall. I doubt it's a coronary. And I'm going to let you diagnose this one.'

He looked at his watch and opened the door. 'Right,' he gave her a small smile, 'let's see if we can beat this morning's speed for the Cord!'

The Cord was the name given to the glassed-in corridor which connected the medical section to the main terminal building. It was about a hundred and fifty yards long, usually free of even pedestrian traffic, and in an emergency it was possible to traverse it in a matter of seconds.

Dr Tranter had long legs and very athletic strides, and Virginia had difficulty in keeping up with him without actually breaking into a run. 'Good girl,' he said, as they reached the door into the main terminal building. 'You remembered the good nurse's maxim—always hurry, but never run. Twenty-eight seconds. Excellent!'

He pushed open the door. After the white antiseptic quiet of the medical section, the noise, the lights, the smells, the bustle of the terminal building burst over them in a scented, discordant, kaleidoscopic wave, and Virginia paused for a moment, blinking her eyes.

Then Dr Tranter touched her arm. 'Main Customs Hall is across and diagonally to the right.' He pointed. 'I'll lead the way.'

Inside the Customs Hall, a large crowd had gathered. 'Right,' Dr Tranter said authoritatively but quietly, 'everyone please stand back—that's it, right back. And you, madam, you'll help your friend more by remaining quiet.'

He waved his hand to disperse the crowd of onlookers who had gathered. To them, the poor woman lying on the floor must have appeared to be very ill. She seemed to be unable to breathe, gasping for air. Her skin was an unhealthy colour and her hands and feet were contorting in catatonic movements.

Dr Tranter dropped to his knees beside her and said in an altered gentler tone, 'Now let's take a good look at you.' He brought out his stethoscope and began his careful examination.

Virginia felt for the patient's pulse and frowned thoughtfully. 'How old is your friend?' she asked the weeping woman behind her.

'Thirty-eight, same as me. Never a day's illness, not to my knowledge. Always been hale and hearty. We'd been on this long weekend to Paris—a treat. She's got a husband and kids, and the men were looking after the kids for us. Whatever shall I tell her husband?'

'Right, Sister!' Dr Tranter whispered something to the patient, then turned, 'I want you to listen to her heart and lungs.' While Virginia did so, he got to his feet and put his hand on the friend's shoulder, murmuring reassuringly in her ear.

'Well, what's your diagnosis, Sister? A coronary?'

'No, Doctor.'

'Then what?'

'She's hyperventilating.'

A faint pleased smile conceded Dr Tranter's approval. Never before had such meagre praise caused Virginia such a feeling of euphoria. 'And do you know the treatment? Can you cure her?'

'Yes, Doctor.'

'Then show me.'

Quickly, from her emergency kit, Virginia brought out a small bag. Then she knelt down beside the patient, put an arm round her shoulders to raise her, and placed the bag over the patient's mouth. 'Blow into the bag,' she told the woman. 'Come on, as hard as you can—all the air you've got in your lungs.' Then she raised the bag over the patient's nose. 'Now inhale. Draw the air in, deeply. Feeling better already? Right, we'll do it again.'

In a while the woman was able to sit in a chair and then stand up.

'Why, it's a marvel, a real marvel!' the friend exclaimed, drying her eyes. 'She's all right. I thought she'd had it, I really did!'

'What came over me, Doctor?' the woman asked.

'Did I have a fit or a heart attack or something awful?'

'No, you didn't. But first we had to make sure. You're a healthy woman,' Dr Tranter told her. 'Tell her what was wrong, Sister.'

'You were breathing too quickly and sending too much oxygen round your bloodstream. You were over-oxygenised, and you needed some carbon dioxide. So the cure is to let you breathe in the carbon dioxide which you expel.'

'But what made me breathe in too much? Why did it come over me?' the woman asked doubtfully, as if she did not quite believe Virginia.

'Ah,' Dr Tranter put in drily, a quirky smile curving his lips, 'that you must ask yourself, madam. It seems you became very nervous.' And with his uncanny perception, or just taking an inspired guess, 'Perhaps,' he raised his brows, 'because you brought in that extra perfume you weren't going to declare!'

The woman's face went suddenly scarlet.

Dr Tranter clicked his tongue reprovingly. There seemed to be nothing, Virginia thought uncharitably, that he liked better than finding a woman in some wrong doing. 'I thought so,' he said. 'Now I suggest you go through the proper Red channel, and pay your custom dues. And let that be a lesson to you!'

'I seem to have heard those words before,' Virginia said to herself when they had returned to the office. She did not repeat them aloud. She had to concede to herself that she had enjoyed the day and she wanted to say nothing that might spoil it. So instead she sat herself down in front of the ledger and began her entry. Once again, to check that each detail was correctly entered in its appropriate column, Dr Tranter came and stood beside her looking over her shoulder. She felt acutely aware of his nearness. She could smell the starched cleanliness of his white coat, a warm masculine smell that was at once reassuring and frightening, and the faint smell of disinfectant from his fingers as he leaned across to point to the disposal column.

'Put "returned home" in that,' he said. 'And you can sign the whole entry. You did it. It was yours. In fact, tomorrow you can do the afternoon calls on your own.' He dropped his hand to her shoulder and patted it absentmindedly, as one might a well-behaved dog.

Yet the gesture warmed her more than extravagant praise. Delighted, she turned to smile up at him, her large grey eyes sparkling with pleasure, a faint flush colouring her fine skin. Just for a moment, he looked at her with a disconcerting intentness, as if he were seeing her for the first time. His dark brows drew together in a frown.

Then suddenly his brow cleared, the straight line of his mouth softened, as his mind apparently turned to pleasanter prospects.

'I shall be along in X-Ray for the next few minutes.' He paused, obviously to think of a viable excuse. 'Clare and I will be giving aircrew medicals tomorrow.' He murmured something about making sure she was all lined up.

He glanced at the clock on the wall. 'Evening Sister will be here in a moment. Don't stay gossiping, get straight off home.' And in the manner of someone conferring chocolate on a child, 'There are still some of Clare's excellent sandwiches left.

Help yourself. You look very tired, you're probably in need of blood sugar.'

It was strange, Virginia thought, hearing the door click shut behind him and his brisk eager step along the corridor outside, that until that moment she had felt remarkably fresh and bright. Now she felt immensely tired, and longing to get back to what was now her home.

'And I want you to feel it's home,' Beryl Best said, spooning on to Virginia's plate a delicious-smelling casserole in which baby carrots and little round onions and garden peas swam in a rich brown beef gravy. 'And how did you make out on your first day?'

'Reasonably well.'

'Think you'll like it?'

'Yes, very much. It's like Casualty, only more so.'

'And the Chief? Think you'll like him?'

Virginia laughed wryly. 'I think he's rather like senior Casualty doctors, only more so.'

'I see.' Beryl picked up her knife and fork and waved to Virginia to begin. 'And the other Sisters? How do you find them?'

'Well, I don't see much of them. It's Box and Cox. Sister Porter, of course, I'd met on my selection board. She's motherly and nice. And Evening Sister, Sister Mortimer, I just met her for a few minutes as I came off. She's an Aussie, very bright and breezy. Comes to work on a moped.'

'Yes, I've met her,' said Beryl. 'She's one of the best—heart of gold. She's married to a chap on an oil rig, isn't she?'

'That's right. Apparently he likes her to work evenings so she won't be tempted to date anyone else.'

'Something to be said for keeping tabs on your partner.' Beryl's eyes strayed to the third place set at the head of the small table. 'But some people . . .' She pursed her lips and choked back what she was going to say. 'I'll put a plateful in the oven to keep hot for Frank.'

'I expect he's working late,' said Virginia.

'Yes,' Beryl agreed soberly, 'I believe they call it that.' She sighed. 'And did you leave Dr Tranter working late?'

'I left him in X-Ray,' Virginia told her.

'That's what I mean.' Beryl put a forkful of food into her mouth and chewed fiercely. 'He was with Clare Todd, I expect. Well, she'd have to be there, wouldn't she? Oh, he wouldn't let her interfere with his work, not the Chief. But it all adds up to the same in the end. He's in love with her. She's his Achilles heel—like this young typist is obviously Frank's.'

'But it may be nothing,' Virginia suggested. 'With Frank, I mean. He may really be busy in the office.'

'So busy that they've been seen out driving together?' Beryl shook her head. 'In the village and in Grantly. *And* parked along a lonely country road, miles from anywhere.' She dabbed her mouth and then surreptitiously her eyes with her napkin. 'Well, don't let's talk about Frank. Now the Chief . . .'

'Oh, don't let's talk about him either,' Virginia sighed. For Beryl, unable to verbalise her misery over Frank, obviously found it therapeutic to talk about someone else.

'I said this morning I'd tell you his problem.'

'You've told me,' Virginia pretended to be absorbed in her supper. 'He's in love with Clare Todd, and no doubt in time he'll marry her. But the sixty-four-dollar question is *when*.'

'You've got a good memory!' Beryl exclaimed approvingly. 'Very good!'

'In my job, you have to,' said Virginia, and felt ashamed, knowing that memory was not the whole truth of it.

'And I'll tell you now why *when* is going to be a while yet.' Beryl drew in a deep breath. 'Miss Clare Todd is engaged to a very famous person.'

'Lucky her! And presumably *unlucky* him. If she's not in love with him, that is.'

'Well, she isn't, not any more. In fact I doubt she ever was. She was carried away, they say, by all the publicity.'

'For what?'

'For him. For Donald Cunningham.'

'The round-the-world yachtsman?' queried Virginia. 'The man who's already won the Transatlantic race?'

'Yes, him. The blond Nordic-looking chap.'

'But isn't he halfway round the world now?'

'Less than half. He'll be away for weeks and weeks yet. They got engaged the day before he set off. It was in all the newspapers and on the telly —champagne party on the yacht, very romantic. You must have seen it?'

Virginia shook her head.

'Rumour has it that Dr Tranter won't announce

their engagement till Donald gets back and Clare can break off *their* engagement properly. Doing the decent thing, it's supposed to be called.'

'It doesn't sound like Dr Tranter,' Virginia protested.

'But you hardly know him!'

'You get to know a person best by working with him. Besides, I formed the impression that he was a man of integrity,' said Virginia.

'My, you are old-fashioned!' Beryl looked at her wonderingly, as if she had stepped out of a Victorian museum. 'No doubt Dr Tranter would say he was acting with integrity.'

'How?'

'Quite easily. If he's in love with a girl, he goes all out to get her, doesn't he? People don't choose to fall in love. And after all, she isn't married to Donald Cunningham, is she? It's not like Frank and this typist girl.'

'I suppose not,' Virginia admitted.

'I don't admire the Chief's choice, but if that's what he wants . . .' Beryl held out her hand for Virginia's plate '. . . let me give you some more.'

'It was delicious, but no, thank you.'

Beryl carried the empty plates through into the kitchen, glancing at the clock on the mantelpiece as she went.

She returned with an apple pie fragrant with cloves and hot Bramley apple juice, and a big brown earthenware teapot. She began serving the pie with angry vigour. As she passed a crock of yellow cream over to Virginia, the clock chimed eight, and Beryl's mouth tightened. As if to concentrate her mind away from Frank's non-appearance, she returned to discussing the Chief. 'After all, you must know what it's like. Haven't you ever been in love?'

'Yes.'

'Well then, you *know*!' Beryl paused in her act of pouring the tea to look soberly across at Virginia. More gently, she asked, 'Didn't it work out?'

'No.'

'All over?'

'He's marrying someone else,' said Virginia flatly.

'Marrying or married?'

'Marrying.'

'Any idea when?'

'In two weeks' time.'

Beryl stared across the table at her shrewdly. Her fine brown eyes looked troubled, her mouth softened. 'You're still in love with him, aren't you?' She blinked as if trying to hold back sympathetic tears. 'Ah, well,' she sighed, 'There's many a slip twixt the cup and the lip. A fortnight's a long time in politics, and a helluva time in our sort of world.'

Virginia pushed back her chair and said firmly, 'I'm not still in love with him. And if it was years instead of weeks, I still wouldn't marry him.'

And on that firm note she announced that she had letters to write and after the washing up would go early to bed. But the conversation with Beryl lingered in her mind. Her sleep was haunted by broken unhappy dreams of Peter with the rich, elegant Antonia. They were both setting off round the world, but the yacht had sprung a leak, and only she could warn them. It was one of those dreams where your limbs are embedded in concrete and when you try to shout no sound comes.

Next morning, she woke with a heavy weight of misery on her chest. She showered and dressed quickly, then went downstairs. Frank must have come in quietly last night, for he was sitting at the breakfast table eating cornflakes with a letter propped against the marmalade pot.

He said 'Good morning. I hope Beryl's made you comfortable,' and returned to his letter without listening to her reply. Virginia doubted if she gave more than a whispered, 'Yes, thank you.' Her eye was caught by a square white envelope set by her own plate. She didn't need to pick it up, or examine the postmark. It was addressed to her in that well-remembered, well-loved handwriting—Peter's. And knowing him as she did, she didn't have to tear open the envelope to know that he was entering her life again.

CHAPTER FIVE

PETER's letter was brief and cryptic. He addressed her as 'My dearest', as he often used to, and continued, 'You promised we would still be friends, and I'm taking advantage of that promise to ask your help. A tricky problem has loomed, and I'd like to discuss it with you. The trouble is, the problem needs resolving with the utmost speed. May I come down and take you out to dinner? Entwick Manor, my spies tell me, is the place. It's very easy for me to get to by train. I'm suggesting Friday at eight-thirty. Come, please, if you can—if not, I'll be there anyway.' It was signed, 'Love as always, Peter,' and there was a PS. 'Had the devil of a job to find the address of your digs.'

It was altogether a puzzling, maddening letter. Virginia re-read it, put it back in its envelope, and helped herself to some cornflakes.

Absentmindedly Frank passed the jug of milk over to her, and she studied his face for a moment. He looked a nice comfortable sort of man, she would have thought, not the unfaithful kind. But then you could never tell.

When Beryl came bustling in with a grilled kipper, Frank drained his cup and pushed back his chair. 'Must be on my way, lovie,' he said to Beryl. He kissed her perfunctorily on the cheek, and added, 'Expect me when you see me.'

'When else?' Beryl answered bitterly, and

clattered the plate down in front of Virginia. And then as Frank opened the front door, she called after him, 'Don't forget I'm going out on service tomorrow—Abu Dhabi.'

'I hadn't forgotten,' Frank said, then he nodded goodbye to Virginia and closed the door.

Beryl turned to Virginia and smiled. 'I'm collecting a plane-load of little perishers coming back to school. I need my head examining! Who would have my job?'

'You would,' Virginia smiled back. 'You love it!'

'Of course I do. It's a hundred times better than housework.'

'Frank seems to take it in his stride.'

'Too much in his stride,' said Beryl bitterly.

'Maybe he misses you.'

Beryl shook her head, and her normally generous mouth set moodily. 'Of course he doesn't. As I told you, Frank has his compensations.'

Virginia said nothing.

'Anyway,' Beryl appeared to recall herself to the present, 'I'll be there and back in the day. Your supper will be in the freezer—Frank's too, *if* he should turn up for it. I'll be home in time to wash up.'

Virginia finished her breakfast, picked up Peter's letter and put it in her handbag. She tried not to think about it, but tried to project her mind to the day ahead. Despite Dr Tranter, she knew the job was exactly the exciting, demanding one that she wanted and needed. She was determined to excel in it. It was too soon to decide what she should do about Peter; Friday gave her ample time to decide. She would put him out of her thoughts till then.

Despite the earliness of her arrival at the medical

section, Dr Tranter was already there. His red light began flashing just as she finished pinning on her cap and before Sister Porter had signed off and donned her cape.

'Ah, Sister Mayhew!' He got up and smiled as Virginia came in, but there was a frosty edge to his smile which should have made her wary. 'Sit down.' He waved her to a chair beside him. 'We'll go through last night's incidents first. Night Sister had quite a busy time one way and another. Usually with less traffic night time is slack.' He pointed, and his shoulder brushed her cheek. 'A young child there covered in chickenpox spots—the poor mother desperate not to miss the holiday. But the aircraft was a charter, mostly of the elderly. Winter sunshine,' he smiled wryly and briefly at Virginia. 'We didn't want to put them at risk of shingles.'

'The grandparents' disease,' Virginia sighed. 'What happened?'

'As you see, Sister Porter coped. The mother was persuaded it was best to put the little girl home in her own bed. She's insured, so she can take the holiday later. You'll get several cases like this —passenger handling, or sometimes the Captain himself will call us in to say they're not happy about a passenger. It's your job and mine to decide if that passenger is fit to travel. If he isn't, you try persuasion first of all, tact. And if that doesn't work you may have to ask the Captain to refuse to take the passenger.'

'I see,' said Virginia. 'And will he?'

'Always. Our word's final.'

Virginia looked up at Dr Tranter's powerful jaw and chin, at the firmly set lips and the uncompromising blue eyes, and thought, Yes, I can well believe that.

'And after that,' Dr Tranter went on, 'a whole run of patients who hadn't had the injections they ought to have had, a chap with severe hypertension who'd left his beta-locks in the train, from the Midlands. Sister had a helluva job getting his GP on the phone! And a nasty one here, suspected case of plague aboard the incoming Singapore flight. The Port Health Authority took over and quarantined.'

Virginia watched Dr Tranter's finger travel down the page. 'We don't as a rule have a post-mortem of the night before,' he said to her as if answering her unspoken question. 'This is just part of your education, get you familiar with the sort of thing you're up against. Now study the rest of them and ask me anything you want. This afternoon, you'll be on call on your own. Clare and I will be doing aircrew medicals.' He gave a little inward-turning smile at the prospect.

Virginia lowered her gaze again to the entries in the incident book. As she read down the column, she was acutely and uncomfortably aware of Dr Tranter's blue eyes on her profile. She tried to think of an intelligent question to ask him, but the entries were so precise and fully annotated that there was nothing she didn't understand.

'Anything you want to ask, Sister?' Dr Tranter raised his brows encouragingly when she looked up at him.

'Not that I can think of, Doctor.'

'Right, then,' he sat back in his chair, 'that takes care of that.' He put the fingertips of both his hands together and stared at them thoughtfully, 'There is one little thing I'd like to ask *you*.' He paused, 'It relates to a phone call that came through just after you left yesterday. A *personal* call.'

'For me?' queried Virginia.

'For you, Sister. Though I took it. The gentleman in question had got PBX to put him through because he said he was a doctor, but when I spoke to him, he wouldn't give his name.'

'How very mysterious!' Virginia said with unaccustomed guile.

'Very,' Dr Tranter agreed. '*More* mysterious in the fact that his voice was very vaguely familiar.' He shot her a sudden glance. 'I rarely forget a voice.'

'I'm sure you don't,' Virginia replied, feeling cornered.

'I thought it could have been this Peter . . . what's-his-name . . .?'

'Willoughby,' she answered much too promptly.

'Willoughby! Ah, yes, thank you.' Dr Tranter wrinkled his brows reminiscently. 'I met him once or twice several years ago.' He looked across at Virginia keenly. 'I wondered if it could have been he?'

She shook her head—that way it seemed not quite an outright lie. Then she added in all truth, 'I hope it wasn't.'

'Good! So do I.' He drew in a deep disapproving breath and went on, 'I took the precaution of telling Rosie not to show anyone through to your office.'

Virginia almost exclaimed aloud at the sheer high-handedness of the man. Living and working as they were in the jet age, he was treating her like some Victorian servant girl, not allowed to have callers! In the taut little silence, her heart seemed to thunder louder than an aircraft taking off over the building.

'Unfortunately, Rosie told me a man had already persuaded her to give him your address.' He smiled a faint wintry smile. 'Rosie is already betting on wedding bells!'

Virginia did not smile. She had the unhappy feeling of treading on slippery and treacherous ground, of not being even distantly in command of the situation. It was a feeling that was unfamiliar to her and therefore more disconcerting and which needed desperate action. If she was to work with Dr Tranter, she had to establish her own independence, the independence she had had no difficulty in maintaining in a busy East London casualty department.

She stood up. As if quite unaware of the tautness of her whole body, of the flush of colour in her cheeks and the dangerous sparkle of battle in her eyes, Dr Tranter said, with the finality of one bringing the matter to a close, 'At least let's hope he doesn't turn up on your doorstep.'

'I'm sure he won't,' said Virginia through stiff lips. 'But if he does, no doubt *you* would like to be informed? Immediately?'

Her heavy sarcasm fell on deliberately deaf ears. Dr Tranter answered, as if blandly unaware of it.

'Yes, do that,' he said with relish. '*I'll* deal with him.'

Virginia put her fingertips on his desk and leaned forward. 'Dr Tranter,' she said in her most decisive and cutting voice, 'does it ever occur to you . . .' She drew in her breath and summoned up her courage to tell him exactly what she thought of him. But before the words came tumbling out, the door was opened and in came Clare, her green eyes suspicious, her mouth reproachful.

'Doctor,' she drawled formally, making the two syllables more caressing than Darling, 'I've still got that wet X-ray for you to see. Will you be much longer?'

Immediately, Dr Tranter's attention was all on Clare.

Virginia felt herself dissolve into the invisible woman. 'Of course, Clare.' He was on his feet. 'I'd quite forgotten,' he tapped his forehead humorously with the open palm of his hand. To Virginia he threw over his shoulder, 'Right, Sister! Let's see how you make out this afternoon.'

Still standing stiff and immobile, Virginia watched them go, he bending his head to hear something Clare whispered, she momentarily resting a hand on his arm. She felt choked with her unuttered defiance. But there were more ways of expressing defiance than mere utterances. She would obey Dr Tranter unswervingly in her professional life. But in her personal life, she owed it to herself to defy him.

Perhaps it wasn't that at all, of course. Perhaps she just wanted to see Peter once more. Whatever it was, there and then she took the decision to accept his dinner invitation.

That evening, lest she change her mind, she wrote a little note to him care of Entwick Manor and delivered it on her way to work the following morning. The note was rather warmer than she might have written earlier: 'Would love to see you again. I'll be there at eight-thirty.'

Dr Willoughby, she was told, had booked a room for Friday night, and was expected around five that afternoon. Rather puzzlingly, he had also booked an adjoining room.

In his name.

Though it was not until Friday evening that Virginia discovered why, the puzzle intrigued her throughout the days that intervened. On her mettle with Dr Tranter, she did not allow it to interfere with one second of her work.

Beryl, delayed in her return from Abu Dhabi, arrived back on the Thursday. She told Virginia, 'I had to make a call at your medical section—a little lassie with a nose that wouldn't stop bleeding. Sister Mortimer was singing your praises, said even the Chief was quite pleased with your work.'

'Praise indeed!' Virginia replied, surprised at the new streak of sarcasm she seemed to have discovered within herself. 'How was the little girl!'

'Fine. They sorted her out a treat. She's on the train now to Brighton and school.'

'You didn't see the Chief himself?'

'He'd just left, cycling off into the wide blue yonder with Miss Todd,' and in the same breath, Beryl asked, 'Did Frank come in for his supper last night?'

'Yes, he did. In fact, when I got home he'd put it in the oven and it was all ready for both of us.'

'And this evening?'

'He went out just before you arrived. Staff meeting, apparently.'

Beryl raised her eyebrows and said, 'Meeting

one of the staff, more likely.'

Virginia shook her head. 'I don't think . . .' she began, but Beryl waved her into silence. 'Let's forget about Frank,' she said. 'Let's have a nice cup of tea and I'll tell you all about my trip.' She kicked off her shoes with a sigh of relief.

'I'll make the tea, Beryl. You stay where you are—here.' Virginia pulled over another chair. 'Put your feet up on this.' She patted Beryl's shoulder as she passed.

She frowned as she set the cups on the tea tray. Just as she would never allow an emotional problem to interfere with her work, so too could she never allow her own problems to lessen her compassion for those of her friends. Already she felt Beryl was her friend, and Frank too. There was no disguising the fact that their marriage was in trouble. Frank had left for that staff meeting showered and spruced and with the eagerness of a young man going to meet his first love. And at the door, aware perhaps of Virginia's worried eyes, he had turned and said, 'Look, my dear, Beryl has her interests and outlets. I've got to have mine.'

Virginia glanced at her watch. It was half past nine and the staff meeting seemed to be continuing. She carried the tray through into the lounge.

Beryl was half asleep.

'Why don't you go to bed? I'll bring the tea up to you there?'

'No, really.' Beryl sat up. 'Not till I've told you all about the trip. I never can sleep till I've unwound. And Frank, as usual, isn't here to listen.' She began sipping the tea Virginia handed her, and said fondly, 'They really were a planeload of little monkeys, up to every trick in the book . . . paint, bagfuls of water, matches! You name it, they got up to it. Luckily the skipper was a friend of mine—an absolute poppet.' Beryl launched on her unwinding, and when Virginia looked at her watch again it was close on midnight. There was still no sign of Frank, but Beryl allowed herself to be bustled off to bed.

'By the way,' Virginia said at Beryl's bedroom door, 'I won't be in for supper tomorrow, I'm going to Entwick Manor.'

Beryl's interest shone through her tiredness, 'He's a lucky fellow! I hope he's worth that light in your eye,' she said, before collapsing exhaustedly on the bed.

Virginia tried not to let any light at all show in her face nor any eagerness in her step as she pushed open the glass revolving doors at Entwick Manor, promptly at eight-thirty, the following evening. But a lurch of the heart and that curious melting weakness of the muscles are luckily totally invisible.

She saw him at once. He was pacing up and down impatiently in the hall. Dear Peter, she thought, he was never prepared to wait for anything or anyone.

He hurried over as soon as she stepped through the doors, both his hands outstretched, head held slightly on one side in that gesture of uninhibited welcome that was so much his.

He took both hers in his grip, and with them imprisoned, kissed her on either cheek, then held her at arm's length and asked in that warm vibrant voice that had helped to win him such a lucrative practice and then made his clinic such a success, 'Dearest, how have they been treating you?' His eyes roamed over her face, light golden brown and full of humorous concern.

Before she could answer, if indeed she had been capable of answering, he answered the question himself. 'Well.' He nodded as if pronouncing a carefully considered diagnosis, 'I really think they have been treating you well. In fact you look wonderful. And I love that blue dress—or is it green? It nearly matches your lovely eyes, clever girl!' He gave her an enthusiastic little kiss on her forehead.

'My eyes are grey,' said Virginia coldly.

'Rubbish!' He pulled her right hand through his arm. 'Now a drink,' he waved her towards a table in the entrance lounge, where a champagne bottle reposed in a silver bucket of ice. 'To celebrate.'

'To celebrate what?' asked Virginia, feeling for some strange reason like someone stone cold sober at a party where everyone else is drunk.

'Ah,' his roguish smile faded, 'there you have me! No, you haven't.' He held out a chair for her. 'To celebrate our meeting up again.' He made it sound an act of Fate.

'But we're meeting for some purpose . . . some problem . . . isn't it? A tricky problem?' Virginia suggested, feeling for the first time ever with Peter that she, not he, was in charge of the situation.

He shot her a look, half affectionate, half irritated. 'Ah yes, dear, dear Ginny, trust you to bring me down to earth!'

Virginia forbore to say that she had not always succeeded in bringing him down to earth. It was a very long time since anyone had called her Ginny in that vibrant, caring way. She watched the waiter uncork the champagne and pour it expertly into the glasses.

'Cheers,' said Peter, raising his glass to eye level and smiling across at her. 'To our meeting.' He drained his glass and held it out to be refilled. He seemed restored to his own effervescent mood again.

'And how has life been treating *you*?' Virginia asked cautiously.

The effervescence subsided.

'Oh, badly. Very badly.' He thrust out his lower lip.

'At work?'

'Oh, no, of course not!' He looked mildly offended, as if she had impugned his professional status. 'My work thrives.'

'In your personal life?'

'Yes, yes, in my personal life.' He ran a hand through his blond hair. 'Why does personal life have to be so complicated? Answer me that, Ginny. Why can't a man do the job he likes and marry the woman he loves and to hell with everyone else?'

'You're a doctor, you should know why,' Virginia said sharply, surprised at what a cool mind she seemed suddenly to have acquired in her dealings with Peter.

He raised his eyebrows. 'Go on,' he said, 'I need your antiseptic good sense.'

'Because life isn't neat and tidy like that. People aren't neat and tidy. Things happen, sometimes awful things. Life is often a succession of problems. Sometimes ones that will never go away.'

'How right you are!' He drained his second glass and waved for the waiter to refill Virginia's. He contemplated the bubbles in silence.

'And you're in the midst of a problem now?' she prompted.

'I am indeed, Ginny—a dire problem, one that will never go away. A six-year-old problem that will outlast *my* life.' He smiled without much humour at her bewilderment. 'In other words, a child. A six-year-old boy.'

Virginia's first reaction was indignation. 'How can you call a child a problem!'

'Oh, easily—very easily. This child I can call the mother and father of all problems.'

'Why?' she queried. 'Is he ill?'

'Lord, no! Healthier than I am.'

'Well then?'

'Because he's Antonia's child. And he hates me.'

Virginia surveyed Peter in silence that clearly irritated him. 'For God's sake,' he exclaimed impatiently, 'you might at least express disbelief! Say, I refuse to believe that! I'm considered to be very good with my child patients.'

'But under the circumstances . . .' Virginia began gently, 'he may well see you as a rival . . .'

'Oh, for heaven's sake! I don't need a lecture on psychology—I've read my Eysenck. Yes, he sees me as a rival all right. And I see him as a *monster*. Does that shock you? Yes, I see it does! Well, that's the truth.'

'And,' Virginia went on doggedly, 'he may have been very attached to his father.'

'What do you mean, may have been? Is, woman! *Is!* Very, *very* attached. And the father is not in the past tense.' Peter drew a deep breath. 'Antonia is a divorcee, not a widow. Yes, I did put it about at the time that she was a widow, but I had my reasons.

The father is still alive, and he too is a monster.'

'Does he . . . the child . . . obviously he has a name . . . ? We can't go on calling him the child . . .'

'Crispin. The monster is called Crispin. Damned silly name!'

'Does Crispin see his father?'

'With disturbing regularity.'

'Presumably the father has access?'

'Yes, of course he has. That's what we're here about.'

Virginia drew in a deep breath. At least now they seemed to have reached the heart of the problem, though how she could possibly help, apart from giving a listening ear, she had no idea.

'The father works in Cairo—our Embassy out there,' Peter told her. 'He's a diplomat, so-called. And the child . . .'

'Crispin.'

'Yes, Crispin goes out to see him, regularly. Believe it or not, the little wretch never wants to come back!'

Half an hour later, when the champagne bottle was empty and the waiter was whispering in Peter's ear that their first course was already on the dining table, Virginia had the complete story, or as near complete as Peter would ever tell her.

Antonia was fond of her son, but she had this high-powered job as a fashion designer and couldn't spare him that much time. The father doted on him, spoiled him, wanted him back. The little wretch was playing one off against the other. And the wedding was less than two weeks away. At eleven, Crispin was arriving back in a party of children, escorted by one of the airline aunts. Antonia was up north at a fashion show, so Peter had been delegated to meet him. They would then stay the night at the Entwick Manor Hotel before going to meet Antonia on her return to her flat.

'As you know,' Peter confided when they had seated themselves at the candlelit table, 'I can't stand scenes. Never could.' He cut up his smoked salmon fiercely. 'Antonia's given me an expensive toy to hand him. And I've booked a damned expensive room next to mine. What more could a child want?'

Virginia said nothing.

'The little monster should be over the moon.' Peter swallowed his food and then asked plaintively, 'But what if he isn't? What if he makes a scene? Do I wallop him, threaten that we won't let him be our page at the wedding?'

Virginia shook her head. 'Neither.'

'Then what?'

'Just try to love him.'

'*Love* him? That child? Impossible!'

Virginia pushed her plate away. She didn't feel hungry any more; she felt as if the sorrows of the world had descended to her shoulders.

For a long time neither of them spoke. Peter watched the roast saddle of lamb being carved with anticipatory relish. When the well filled plate was in front of him and the silence still unbroken, he looked across the table.

'Well, say something,' he ordered, and with a return of the roguish smile she used to love, 'If it's only *serve you right*.'

'That's the last thing I'd say.'

'I know, dearest, I know. You never were one to kick a chap when he's down.'

He paused to watch two people being shown to the table behind Virginia, looking up at them half smiling.

'But I do think,' she spoke the words slowly, 'that you've both . . . Antonia and you . . . got to do a lot of thinking before . . . well, before you marry . . . I mean, do you have to marry in two weeks . . . could you give Crispin more time . . . to get used to you?' The trouble was it sounded like a suggestion and an invitation, a suggestion that he postpone the wedding and perhaps by implication see more of her. She coloured at her own clumsiness. But Peter seemed pleased and even reassured at her words. He nodded.

'You're so right!' he said, 'so very right. As you say, Antonia and I mustn't rush into things. It wouldn't do any harm to postpone the wedding, and it might do a lot of good.' He sighed and leaned across the table to whisper, 'And could I ask you one small favour?'

'Of course.'

'Come with me to the airport to meet the little monster.'

'Tonight?' she queried.

'Yes, why not?'

'But would it do any good? He might hate me too.'

'I've yet to meet the child that did,' Peter smiled gallantly. 'Will you try it? Just to please me?'

'If you think it would help.'

'I know it would. Bless you!' He seized both her

hands with such vigour that she dropped her knife with a clatter to the floor. She bent to retrieve it.

The hand of the man sitting back to back with her was also searching for the knife. She touched his fingers, then they fastened over hers, and she turned her head further.

She saw the dinner-jacketed arm of the man behind her. Her gaze travelled upward, and she looked up into the angry blue eyes of Dr Richard Tranter.

'Why, Sister Mayhew!' Dr Tranter stood up, those blue eyes sparkling, his tone mocking. He looked, she thought, unfairly handsome in the well cut dinner suit. Then he moved a step to stand by their table, disclosing that the woman opposite him was, as Virginia would have expected, Clare Todd. 'And isn't that Willoughby?' He drew down his brows with manifest disapproval.

Virginia flushed with anger and discomfort. The Chief could so easily have ignored their proximity, but there he was forcing himself in on them.

'Yes,' Peter jumped to his feet. 'Yes, it is, sir.' He sounded deferential, which he usually did to more senior doctors. 'You've got a good memory, sir! I didn't expect you to remember me. I think I was briefly a junior houseman when you were Casualty Registrar.'

The Chief nodded but made no comment. 'Clare, my dear, may I introduce Dr Willoughby? Sister Mayhew, of course, you already know.' The Chief put his hand on Clare's shoulder. He didn't call her his fiancée or friend or anything, just Clare. Peter, taking Clare's hand, looked suitably dazzled

—and dazzling indeed she was, dressed in a décolletée gown of emerald velvet, that showed off the creamy skin of her shoulders and neck. The only jewellery she wore was long thin emerald ear-rings that glittered against the magnificent rich red of her hair.

'Forgive me,' Peter said to her in his most humble voice. 'I know it's very rude to remark on it, but your gown is *so* becoming, I feel I must tell you how wonderful you look.'

'Thank you, Doctor.' Clare's expression melted.

'A friend of mine,' Peter went on to explain, 'is a fashion designer, so I'm an amateur expert, if there is such a beast.'

'A friend? Your fiancée, surely?' Dr Tranter corrected drily.

Peter looked momentarily discomfited. But he went on to enquire where Miss Todd had found such a creation, and after several minutes, while the men stood and the waiters hovered, Peter suggested artlessly, 'Look, sir, why don't we join forces—put our tables together? They're already almost together.'

'I think not,' Dr Tranter said firmly. 'We have to leave early.

He sounded very forbidding. Undoubtedly, Peter's flirting with Clare had fuelled his anger. Virginia could feel it, palpable as heat through the thin silk of her dress as the men resumed their places, Dr Tranter sitting back to back with her again, a strange posture, it seemed to her, of intimacy and rejection.

Virginia wished the restaurant were not so crowded. Now she knew he was there, back to back wasn't good enough; he was far too uncomfortably close. She could hear every tinkly laugh from Clare Todd, and more disturbingly Dr Tranter's deep, slow, manifestly enjoying one.

With relief, at about ten o'clock, she heard Dr Tranter ask the waiter for his bill. Clare came and stood beside their table to bid Peter goodnight. Dr Tranter gave them a curt nod, and added to Virginia, 'Don't be late home. We have a busy day tomorrow.'

'Always was a slavedriver,' Peter remarked to her sympathetically when they had gone. 'Good doctor, though, I suppose you can say. So people put up with it—they wouldn't otherwise.'

Virginia said nothing. She drank her coffee and watched Peter eat his peppermint creams with relish.

'I suppose we should start making tracks soon, though,' he went on. 'The aircraft's due in at eleven. Shall we get a taxi or use your car?'

'We'll use mine,' she smiled. 'It knows the way.'

'Not still your old banger!' he exclaimed as they settled themselves in ten minutes later. 'I'd have insisted on the taxi if I'd known,' he smiled.

'Perhaps Crispin will enjoy it as a vintage car,' she suggested lightly, as she put the key in the ignition.

'Ah, Crispin,' he groaned. 'Yes, Crispin. Don't remind me! I'd managed to forget about the little beast for a blessed hour or two.'

'Well, you can't,' said Virginia, coaxing the engine to fire and releasing the handbrake.

Peter stared moodily out of the window and said nothing. He seemed unmoved and unexcited by the myriad many-coloured lights of the airport, a township of stars, Virginia thought, with other stars, red and green and white, circling in the bright sky above them. When they pulled up outside the Passenger Terminal, she said, 'I'll go and park the car, while you wait for him at Arrivals. I won't be long. And it might be best if he saw you first.'

'It won't be, I promise. He's allergic to me. So hurry! I tell you I can't cope with him on my own.'

Ten minutes later, having parked the car, Virginia found Peter pacing impatiently up and down the passenger hall smoking furiously. He pointed to the television screen of Arrivals. 'There it is—782 from Cairo, landed. He won't be long now. Why did I let myself in for this?'

'Presumably,' said Virginia, 'because you love Antonia.'

'Yes, I suppose you're right.' Peter ground out his cigarette. 'But there's a limit.' He scowled at the still closed doors of Customs through whose shadowy frosted glass anonymous figures could be seen moving.

Suddenly the doors opened and out came the first trickle of passengers triumphantly pushing trolleys of souvenirs and duty-free goods, and scanning the waiting people behind the ropes, for familiar faces.

After a few seconds the doors opened again. Virginia heard a little explosion of excited young voices, and there emerged a tall thin woman in the brown and gold uniform of an airline aunt. She had a child on either side of her, talking eagerly, and two older children walking behind. They all wore the white medallions.

'Which one is Crispin?' asked Virginia, standing on tiptoe.

'Can't see him yet.'

Virginia noticed that someone who looked like a proud grandmother was standing not far from Peter and herself waving to the children, and that all four were waving back happily to her.

She was just about to say, 'I'll go and ask the aunt,' when from under her arm the aunt brought out a piece of cardboard with *Dr Willoughby* written on it. She began waving it invitingly above her head.

Peter raised his arm and over she came, her kind middle-aged face crumpled and worried. 'Oh, Dr Willoughby,' she exclaimed, 'I'm so sorry, but I have a disappointment for you. We haven't been able to bring Crispin. He made such a scene at Cairo airport that his father flatly refused to let him come with us. There was nothing we could do. We did our best. Mr Villiers promised he would see he came in a day or so. But I hope you're not too distressed and disappointed.'

Rising to the occasion, as always, Peter made the right replies. He even managed to look bravely disappointed. Then when the aunt had disappeared he slipped his hand through Virginia's arm and said, 'Now I think we *do* have something to celebrate! Another few days without the monster—and you and me together again!'

He seemed truly disappointed only when Virginia merely dropped him off at the hotel, refused a nightcap, refused a goodnight kiss and returned to her bed-sitting room, there to brood on the sad fate of young Crispin and the heartlessness of two grown men.

CHAPTER SIX

FOR in her opinion, Peter's heartlessness was not all
that much greater than the Chief's. Virginia crept
in quietly to Number Seven that night. She took off
her best blue dress and hung it on the hanger. How
dowdy, she thought, it must have looked in com-
parison with Clare Todd's ravishing green creation.

The house was quiet, but she found it difficult to
sleep. It was a warm and sultry night. The airline
summer schedule was still under way and the great
arch of the sky reverberated to the sound of aircraft
engines. She had drawn back her curtains when she
switched off the light, and she could see those
brooches of red and green and white aircraft lights
as they carved their way across the stars.

She threw back the bedclothes, she punched her
pillows, but sleep refused to come. Her mind kept
going in circles like the aircraft above her head. She
kept thinking of young Crispin and Peter who
disliked him, and then round to the Chief who so
obviously disliked Peter. She remembered, with
piercing clarity, the angry expression in the Chief's
blue eyes. She thought, with dread, of the coming
day. Would the Chief mention last night, or would
he ignore the whole episode? She couldn't decide
which she would find worse.

When she took over from Monica Porter the next
morning, the Senior Sister paused in their perusal
of the medical log to remark that Virginia looked

pale. She clicked her tongue like a mother hen and went on reprovingly, 'Too many late nights, my dear. The Chief said only a few moments ago that he thought you might be burning the candle at both ends.'

'So he's in already, is he?' Virginia asked nervously.

'In, but not in the section. He's gone round to do a spot check on the catering kitchens.'

'Busy man, our Chief,' Virginia remarked drily.

But Sister Porter took the remark at its face value. 'Indeed he is, very busy. When you think of all he has to deal with besides airport health!'

'He's got Dr Lascelles for nights, and the Grantly practice to call in.'

'Ah, but the Chief always likes to keep a finger on all the pulses.'

'And in all the pies,' Virginia thought resentfully, but not aloud.

Aloud, she said, 'The sections must dread these spot checks.'

'Oh, they know it's for everyone's good. And the Chief does it so nicely that they never mind.' Sister Porter began to slip on her cape. 'As you see, hc's checked the medical log with me and we've both signed it. And he's left a note for you.' She brought a folded piece of paper out of her pocket and handed it to Virginia. 'I must go—my hubby's here.'

Virginia unfolded the piece of paper. 'You're on your own,' it said in the Chief's clear handwriting. 'I shall be giving aircrew medicals all day. Call me if there's anything you can't cope with.'

Virginia crumpled the note and threw it into the wastepaper basket. Relief that she would not be seeing Dr Tranter probably till tomorrow, by which time the dinner at Entwick Manor might well be forgotten, mingled with a healthy determination that there would be nothing and no one with whom she couldn't cope.

She had coped with a busy London casualty department; she could cope with this strangely exciting and different place.

Before the phone had a chance to ring, she checked with a certain proprietorial pride that her section was ship-shape. It was all so like a mini-ature, very up-to-date hospital—the same glitter-ing white and chrome, the same antiseptic smells. The well-equipped treatments room, the tiny emergency ward with its life-support machine, the little waiting room, the Sister's office, could have been straight out of her past. Even the ringing of the emergency telephone and the flashing of warning lights was familiar.

What wasn't familiar yet, she thought, what was still exciting and mystifying and challenging was what happened after the phone rang and the lights flashed; when, checking her bleeper and her ID card and radio token, she hurried down the Cord to a different jet-age city where almost anything could have happened.

And today she would do it on her own.

The first emergency call of the morning came as she was checking the sterile dressings. 'Sister,' a man's voice requested urgently, 'can you come quick—bay Two, Airside. Chap with his hand crushed in the lift gates.'

'Is he conscious?' she asked.

'Just about.'

Pausing only to push the emergency call bell through to Rosie, Virginia picked up her emergency bag and sped down the Cord, hardly glancing at the beginnings of a fine late summer day, her mind totally on what lay ahead. She hurried through the crowded Arrivals area and was wafted, a Freeman now of this great buzzing city, through towards Airside. There she unlocked the security doors with her radio token as with a wand, and reached the anxious little knot of people standing by the service lift, where a man in blood-stained white overalls was sprawled on a chair. His mate was trying clumsily to staunch the blood and, as he said, 'Keep his pecker up.'

'You're a sight for sore eyes,' the patient croaked. 'My mate's not got much of the gentle touch.' He tried to make a joke as he watched Virginia fill a hypodermic syringe. 'I never thought I'd look forward to getting the needle!'

Which was another thing, she thought, as she dabbed his arm before the injection, how heart-warmingly brave people were, how these emergencies seemed to bring out the best in them. She was beginning to discover too that she had a knack of being able to talk to total strangers and sense their problems without their having to speak them. She felt the man's anxious eyes on her face as she examined his hand. 'It's all right,' she said, 'you don't have to worry. But I do think you'll be best in hospital.'

'You always was the lucky one,' his mate told him, still trying valiantly to cheer him. 'Think of all them lovely nurses! Pretty as Sister, I shouldn't wonder.'

But the patient was already drifting off, and by the time the ambulance carried him away to the County Hospital down the road, Virginia's bleeper was sounding. A woman in the Ariel Restaurant was choking on a fishbone, and when Sister had dealt with that, her presence was earnestly requested at the Singapore Airlines check-in, where a young woman passenger had fainted.

Some time later, Virginia returned down the Cord, the fishbone successfully removed, the young woman revived and seemingly in the early stages of pregnancy.

The sun was high in the sky above now, turning the aircraft in the circuit to great silver fish in a vast upturned bowl of blue. It glittered on the glass of the Cord, transforming it to crystal. On that return journey, not so frantically hurried and content with her work so far, Virginia allowed herself the luxury of looking out on either side.

The Cord seemed to have been designed to act like a crystal ruler between Airside and Groundside. Airside were the runways, the taxiways, the vast expanse of grass, the hangars, the Control Tower, the parking piers for the aircraft. Virginia had intended to count the number of steps down the Cord and how long it took her, but there were so many interesting things happening outside on Airside that she lost count. A jumbo jet lumbered over the road and over her head to land unerringly between the long rows of yellow runway lights; a helicopter seemed to fall straight out of the sky to land on the pad just outside.

On the road itself, Virginia saw a white convertible, that could only belong to Clare Todd. Its hood was down and it was being driven at some speed towards the workshops and offices of Groundside. She caught a glimpse of Clare's red-gold hair streaming prettily behind her, saw the gardener tending the flower beds in between the roads straighten to admire her, before the car disappeared behind their own medical section.

Minutes later, when Virginia arrived there, Rosie opened her Reception window to whisper, 'The Chief's just been by to see if you're keeping your head above water. He says to give him a buzz if you need him. He's in his office now, and Clare's with him.'

'Thank you,' Virginia smiled. As she passed the Chief's door, she heard the sound of Clare's voice, and her tinkly laugh, and a sudden exclamation, 'Oh, Richard, I'm so happy! You've no idea how happy.'

Frowning, Virginia went into her own office, closed the door, scrubbed her hands and rang for her first patient without allowing herself to speculate on what had made Miss Clare Todd so happy.

It was ten to four before the last patient departed and she had time to check the medical log. She could hear Sister Mortimer's moped puttering outside, as she put her signature at the end of the page. She ran her hand through her dark wavy hair and sat for a moment with her hands clasped in front of her, her grey eyes troubled.

Despite the Chief's manifest doubts, she had coped. Yet she felt none of the usual satisfaction of a day's work well done. The friendliness of the people at the airport no longer seemed to warm her heart, and she felt instead a curious ache inside herself compounded of many sharp and niggling pains. The rewards of the day's work faded, and her thoughts returned to the worries of last night again.

Crispin was the most pressing worry. What would become of the child? And his father, what would *he* do? Would he make Crispin return to his mother? And would she marry Peter? Presumably, poor Mrs Villiers was torn between Crispin and Peter. How was she going to resolve it? And Peter himself, despite his heartlessness, what would happen to him?

But beyond these worries, there was another pain. It was a selfish pain and an unworthy one. When she forced herself to drag it out into the open, she saw just how unworthy it was. The source of the pain was Dr Tranter, his high-handed arrogant treatment of her last night, contrasting so sharply with the smooth, happy way he seemed to have worked with Clare Todd. 'Oh, Richard, I'm so happy!' Why did she have to overhear that remark, Virginia asked herself, and what had Dr Tranter just said to make Clare Todd utter it?

At that point, after the most perfunctory of knocks, the object of her speculation put his head round the door, and Virginia felt her cheeks flush a guilty scarlet.

'Have you coped all right, Sister?' Dr Tranter asked with polite formality.

'Yes, thank you, Doctor,' Virginia answered, searching his face. Though she tried to tell herself firmly that this professional enquiry was the sole object of his visit, her female intuition told her otherwise.

Her female intuition was right. Richard Tranter stepped into her office and with a slow and deliberate movement closed the door behind him.

'So,' he said in the same formal tone he had used before, 'you chose to ignore my advice about Willoughby?' He leaned on the panels of the door, with his hands thrust deep into the pockets of his white coat, one questioning eyebrow raised.

Virginia drew in a deep breath. When Dr Tranter had lectured her on Peter Willoughby before, she had intended to make clear to him that he had no right to interfere in her private life. Now his carelessly arrogant manner, his cool assumption of authority over her private life, made her recognise that this time she must stand up for herself.

The thought made her do exactly that. She got to her feet and drew herself to her full five feet two inches. 'Yes, Doctor,' she said. 'As your advice was personal and not professional I have every right to ignore it.'

He stared at her unhurriedly for a moment, then he came and stood in front of her desk, looking down at her from his own considerable height. 'Oh, yes,' he said evenly, 'everyone has the right to be foolish. But one is supposed to learn.'

'I was not being . . .' she began, and then in all honesty stopped. Foolish was of course exactly what she had been.

He noticed her hesitation and smiled, not unkindly. 'At least you admit that.'

'I'm *admitting* nothing.' Virginia tilted up her chin.

Ignoring her angry exclamation, he went on as if allowing extenuating circumstances, 'And I'm sure it was *Willoughby* who got in touch with *you*.'

'How very perceptive of you!' Virginia exclaimed.

He answered her sarcasm with a nod, continuing, 'But you foolishly allowed yourself to be persuaded. I suppose he wanted to renew the acquaintance. Or did he want to cry on your shoulder?'

'Certainly not! Neither,' she protested loyally. She straightened her shoulders and said with dignity, 'He simply wanted the advice of an old friend.'

'Which you were only too eager to give.'

'*Willing* to give.'

'In fact you advised him not to rush into marriage?'

Virginia drew in her breath sharply. 'I shan't answer that. It's nothing to do with you!'

'My dear girl, I heard you.'

'Then why ask?' Her eyes sparkled. 'And how dare you listen to our conversation? To eavesdrop?' She clenched her fists. She could not remember when she had felt so painfully angry.

'I had no choice *but* to hear your conversation,' Richard Tranter said coolly. 'You'll recall that we were sitting very close, back to back. And you, Sister, spoke with great clarity and conviction. From the heart, one might say.' He drew a deep breath as if he was about to say more. But at that point Sister Mortimer came in, carrying her crash helmet under one arm and a nursing journal under the other. She had just been reading an article, she said, about some new pills patented in America, that were said to counteract jet-lag. What did Dr Tranter think? she asked cheerfully, oblivious of the tension in the office.

Thankfully, Virginia made her escape.

She did not, however, escape questioning about last night altogether. Beryl had been into the Airline Escort Service office and had learned about Crispin.

She brought Virginia a tray of tea and some home-made biscuits and said, 'Really, Virginia, you could have knocked me down with a feather when I heard *you* were at the airport last night. And with Crispin's stepfather!'

'His stepfather-to-be. He's not married to Crispin's mother yet.'

'You never mentioned you were going to the airport,' Beryl said reproachfully.

'Because I didn't know I was going.'

'Dinner at Entwick Manor, *you* said.'

'And dinner only I thought it was going to be,' Virginia explained. 'The airport was rather sprung on me.'

Beryl looked only half mollified. 'Do you realise,' she said severely, 'that Crispin is the first child we've ever failed to deliver?'

'No, I didn't.' Virginia took a sip of tea. 'He's spoiled the service's fine unblemished record, has he?'

Beryl nodded. 'Not that I blame you, of course. Not that anyone blames you. How could they? You were just an innocent bystander. In fact, I don't see how you came into it. Though I've given it a lot of thought. This Dr Willoughby who was meeting Crispin is the one you're carrying a torch for, isn't it? The one you hoped to marry? The one you're in love with?'

'No,' said Virginia, and put down her cup. 'No, I don't think I'm still in love with him.' She tried that concept in her mind like trying on a new pair of shoes. The concept only pinched a little. 'No,' she repeated, 'I don't think I still love him. I think I feel sorry for him. And he wanted me to help him.'

'And does he need help!' Beryl exclaimed, rolling her eyes expressively towards the ceiling. 'Or so I'm told.'

'Because of young Crispin?'

'Because of Crispin and himself, and Crispin's mother and father.'

'Oh.'

'Mostly because of himself,' Beryl added weightily.

'How do you know? You've never met him.'

'I had a long, long talk with Phoebe—she was the aunt on duty.'

'She saw very little of Peter,' Virginia assured her.

'My, my, we are defensive, aren't we?' Beryl laughed.

'I'm merely pointing out a fact. Phoebe simply came over to Peter to apologise for Crispin's absence. She can't be that quick a judge of character.'

'Oh, but she is!' Beryl replied stubbornly. 'All of us aunts are. Besides, she had a long talk with Crispin, and an even longer one with Crispin's father.'

'Who would be very biased.'

'Very worried, more like—worried to death,

Phoebe said. He simply adores the child.'

'And the child himself? Crispin? What did Phoebe say about him?'

'Phoebe loves all children,' Beryl replied diplomatically.

'So even she reckons he's difficult?'

'She didn't say so.'

'Peter reckons he's a handful,' Virginia said.

Beryl shrugged. 'He would.' Then she smiled mysteriously. 'Anyway, I shall soon find out. Muggins here is being sent out to collect young Crispin.' She rolled up the sleeves of her jumper and flexed her non-existent muscles. 'Don't look so hopeful —Dr Willoughby won't be meeting him. The office has arranged that his mother will be at the airport.'

'And when do you go?'

'Oh, not till next week. Frank will have to put up with another frozen dinner.' Automatically, as she always did when she spoke of Frank, Beryl allowed her eyes to stray to the clock. 'Working late again!' she exclaimed bitterly. 'If only Frank got paid overtime, I'd be on Easy Street.'

'Perhaps he gets lonely without you,' Virginia pointed out.

'Don't you believe it! He *enjoys* himself without me.' Beryl frowned at the clock.

'And do you think you'll succeed with Crispin?' Virginia endeavoured to draw Beryl's attention away from Frank's lateness.

'Oh, I think so,' she said. 'Frank is just about the only little boy I can no longer charm.'

CHAPTER SEVEN

FOR the rest of the week and the beginning of the next, Frank continued to work late. Beryl's mouth tightened, her eyes grew more suspicious. To Virginia's relief Peter neither telephoned nor wrote. While Richard Tranter maintained a cool aloof professional manner towards her, as the tempo of life at the airport accelerated with the holidaymakers coming home.

Called out several times a day, Virginia began to know the bewildering streets of the jet-age city at the other end of the Cord, where everything was, and what everybody did. Ken Milner-Brown introduced her to some of the traffic officers. She got to know the Minister of the little chapel on the second floor, because he sometimes came to an emergency to see if there was anything he could do. She met controllers and loaders and cleaners, and remembered them by name. Airport policemen became names, too, not just blue uniforms.

Through the bustle and sometimes frenzy—Entwick on a Saturday was as crowded as a Cup Final—there was always that link, the cheery raised hand, the salute, the smile, the 'Nice morning' or the 'Cheerio, Sister'. At least, there was from everyone but Dr Tranter.

Increasingly, too, the world beat a pathway to her door. The waiting room was filled up every day with walking cases. 'You've acquired the reputation,' Beryl told her over breakfast the following

Thursday morning, 'of having a gentle pair of hands—fatal! Your predecessor had a very rough hand with the needle. No one ever forgot to have their injections done by their GP when she was on.'

Virginia smiled. 'I don't believe you.'

'Well, shall we say she didn't draw the customers in like you seem to. Anyway, don't overwork while I'm away.'

She was off that morning to collect the formidable Crispin. She had the white disc ready to give him. The boy's father had undertaken that this time there would be no difficulties.

'He's promised the lad'll come quietly,' Beryl said, buttoning up her smart caramel-coloured jacket. 'And his mother has promised faithfully to be at the Arrivals barrier to meet him in.'

'And Peter Willoughby?' queried Virginia. 'Is he going to meet him as well?'

'Well, our department suggested, ever so tactfully, mind, that it might be as well if he didn't.'

'I agree,' said Virginia.

'You're not disappointed?'

'Quite the reverse.'

Beryl looked disbelieving, but didn't argue. She accepted Virginia's offer of a lift to the airport, so that she would have time to collect comics and games and toys from what was known as the aunts' 'magic chest' to keep Crispin occupied from Cairo to London.

Dr Tranter's bicycle was not in its customary place, nor was Clare Todd's, but there was a white BMW which Beryl identified as the Chief's. 'He'll have given her a lift in, I shouldn't wonder.' she said. 'I suppose you heard the lone yachtsman was sighted a week ago, but since then he's been out of radio contact.'

Virginia shook her head.

'Well, he has, poor chap. It was on the late night news. But there, life's full of problems. Wish me luck with *my* particular problem, will you? Crispin, I mean, not Frank.'

She brought out of her pocket the white disc with its message UNACCOMPANIED. PLEASE HELP and surveyed it with a wistfulness that was not, Virginia knew, entirely for Crispin.

'Yes,' Virginia said gently. 'Good luck. I'm sure you'll manage. See you this evening. What time are you due back?'

'Sixteen hundred. It's a quick turn round.'

'Well, I'll put Frank's dinner in the oven if you're delayed.'

Two hours later, Virginia forgot about Crispin. She was immersed in her clinic dealing with a waiting room full of patients—a policeman with athlete's foot, or Mango Toe as he preferred to call it, a foreman with conjunctivitis, a loader who'd strained his back, a marshaller with chest pains and a whole series of passengers who had missed their injections. Then an urgent call came from Lost Property to say an old lady was asking if her angina pills had been handed in, and this was followed by a request to go to the Spectators' Gallery where a baby was having convulsions.

Shortly after a hasty lunch, as she made her entries in the medical log, Richard Tranter came in and stood behind her. 'I'll do the rest of the outside emergency calls today,' he told her. 'We've finished medicals. I've a lecture to give to the cabin crew on

Survival, but that's not till four-thirty.'

He frowned, drawing his dark brows down moodily, as if the thought of survival reminded him of the lone yachtsman, or perhaps that was all Virginia's imagination, and his frown was no more than an expression of his dislike at giving formal lectures.

And then he saw that the frown was directed at herself. 'You look pale,' he said, scrutinising her face. He leaned over and pulled down the lower lid of her eye. 'Are you tired?'

'Not really.'

'That means yes.' He sighed. 'Well, cut off home directly Sister Mortimer comes. You haven't many patients in the waiting room.' And after a pause, 'Remember, a tired nurse is rarely a good nurse.'

'I'm not really tired,' she protested.

Dr Tranter probed further. 'Are you finding the responsibility too much?'

'Certainly not!'

He smiled slightly at her vehemence. 'Are you worrying about anything then?'

Virginia opened her mouth to say that she had no immediate worries, apart perhaps from young Crispin, for whom she felt indirectly responsible, but that might lead to the subject of Peter Willoughby; and something warned her it would be unwise to remind Dr Tranter of him.

So she shook her head, and shrugging his shoulders as if he had no intention of forcing her confidence, Dr Tranter lifted the telephone and told PBX to put all emergency calls through to him.

He left her office without another word.

It seemed oddly empty when he had gone.

Virginia sat for several seconds brooding over that fact. Then a soft apologetic knock sounded on her door. Absentmindedly, she called 'Come in,' and round the door, only about halfway up, came a little bald-headed man, his rosy face wreathed in an apologetic smile.

'Sorry to trouble you, Sister. I'm Lowry the Lamp, and one of my big boys has backfired.'

Virginia had already discovered that in this strange glittering jet-age city, it was quite customary, as in some little villages in Wales, for people to get known by their occupation. It was a term of affection and a means of identification.

'Come in, Mr Lowry, and let me take a look at you,' she smiled.

He came in cautiously with his right hand behind his back. 'It's not a pretty sight, Sister. Makes me think of the Red Hand of Ulster!'

'Then let's go through into the treatments room and see what we can do.'

As she unwound the blood-soaked bandages, and removed the glass splinters, she heard how he had been removing one of the big bulbs, 'when it went phut in my hand.'

'I'm in charge of all the bulbs at Entwick,' he told her. 'Guess how many we've got?'

'Five thousand?' she suggested tentatively, remembering what a city of sparkling lights it looked at night.

'*Twenty* thousand, Sister.'

'It must be a big responsibility?'

'Certainly is. Especially the runway lights. Can't have them going off, can we? It'd be worse than a lighthouse going out.'

'So it would be,' she agreed.

'And when you think that aircraft weighing three hundred tons come down on them at a hundred and forty knots . . . well, you can imagine.'

Virginia looked suitably impressed. She had seen the big yellow runway lights, the green threshold lights, and the blue lights edging the taxiways many times, and thought how beautiful they looked. But she had never paused to think there was someone hidden in an office in the vast complex whose job it was to maintain such a flawless display.

'Well now, Mr Lowry, we'll look at those cuts under another of your lamps, before I dress them.' She smiled at him.

Then she asked him about his anti-tetanus injections, scolding him when she discovered they were not up to date. She made a joke about *his* own health maintenance being as important as his lamps, gave him a booster and an antibiotic, then told him to come back in two days' time and waved him goodbye.

Just about now, she thought, sitting back in her chair, and looking at the clock, Beryl's aircraft should be approaching over Mr Lowry's green approach lights. In about an hour, if she had been successful in bringing Crispin back, she should be handing him over to his mother. What would take place after that, Virginia couldn't guess. She hoped Peter would try to understand the child; she hoped the child would eventually take to him. Nevertheless, they should give Crispin time to adjust emotionally. She had been right, surely, to advise Peter not to rush into marriage? She hadn't had an ulterior motive, as Dr Tranter had so unforgivably suggested.

At the thought of Dr Tranter's remarks, Virginia's mind came to a rebellious halt. He had no right to impute such selfish, devious motives to her, and certainly no right to interfere in her private life. She pressed the buzzer for the next patient to come in, thrusting the thoughts of Crispin and Peter and her resentment of Dr Tranter to the back of her mind. But they didn't go away.

When Dr Tranter strode into her office on the heels of Sister Mortimer, and bade Virginia in a brisk no-nonsense tone to 'Get off home', she thought angrily, 'I'm just about as important to him as one of Mr Lowry's lamps! He doesn't want me to go phut, because it would be a chore to replace me, but replace me he would. The work must go on.'

And though something deep inside herself recognised that that interpretation was not totally fair, she knew she dared not explore her own judgments and feelings too deeply. Her anger somehow protected her from Richard Tranter. She hugged it to her.

As she walked towards the car park, she caught a glimpse of him through his large office window. He was taking off his white coat and shouldering his way into his jacket. Virginia saw his face in profile, the straight nose, the firm lips, the powerful jaw. She got into her car and pulled the door shut behind her with finality, as if shutting out with it that glimpse of Dr Tranter.

She pushed the key in the ignition and turned it quickly—too quickly. The old starter, used to her more gentle handling, groaned its protest. She tried again, and again it refused to forgive her.

In the driving mirror, she saw that Dr Tranter had

appeared in the doorway of the medical section. He was carrying a file under his arm, and an oblong slide box. To her horror, she saw him saunter down the steps and make a beeline towards her.

'Don't let me down,' she breathed, turning the key in the ignition once more and willing the engine to fire. 'Please!'

This time it obliged her. She pressed on the accelerator, and was just about to release the hand-brake, when the passenger door was opened.

Dr Tranter suggested, pleasantly enough, 'You'll be passing the Lecture Hall, would you be kind enough to give me a lift?'

To anyone else, Virginia would have smiled and agreed willingly. But it wasn't anyone else: it was Richard Tranter.

She heard herself say contentiously, 'If you trust my driving.'

His blue eyes crinkled up. 'Let's say it's time I gave it another try.' He climbed in, folding up his long legs, and putting the slide box between his feet. The file he cradled on his lap. 'And anyway, this lecture stuff is awkward on a bike.'

'At least it isn't far,' Virginia said, as much to herself as Dr Tranter.

'Exactly,' he agreed, watching her reverse and turn on to the hangar road, and then on to the main Groundside road, after giving due heed to the dotted white lines at the intersection.

At the Lecture Hall, Dr Tranter got himself and his impedimenta out. 'Thanks,' he said, and with a quizzical gleam in his blue eyes, added, 'Your driving is improving.' His mouth relaxed into one of his rare oddly boyish grins. 'We stopped a full minute at the white lines.'

'I'm glad you noticed,' Virginia said coldly.

'Noticed? I thought you were going to tell me we'd run out of gas.'

Virginia laughed. Just for a moment, their profiles were turned to one another, smiling and relaxed.

Then he looked at her more intently. His smile faded and his mood changed. In his old brusque manner, he said, 'Well now, off you go.' He slammed the car door and called through the open window, 'Straight home!'

She didn't go straight home. Indeed, it gave her some faint pleasure to defy him. It made her feel protected from him, less vulnerable. She had several calls to make before she returned to Number Seven—some shoes to pick up from the menders, a suit to take into the dry-cleaners at Grantly. These small tasks gave her time to distance herself from that short, rather bewildering encounter with Richard Tranter. Finally, before heading for home, she paid a visit to the florist's and chose a bunch of flowers for Beryl to cheer her after what would have been a stressful trip with Mrs Villiers' child.

Carrying her large bunch of pink carnations, gift-wrapped and tied with a big matching bow, Virginia put her key in the door.

The sight that met her eyes kept her rooted to the spot. The normally scrupulously neat sitting room was upside down. Furniture was overturned. Blankets and bedspreads and some of Beryl's beautiful linen tablecloths were draped over the upended tables. It was as if a bomb had hit the place. Virginia put down her flowers, and looked round aghast. Her first thought was that the house had been burgled. She looked for a broken window or signs of a forced entry.

Then she heard from under one of the blankets a most peculiar sound, like a yelp of childish laughter. The blanket wriggled as if it were alive, and from under it, a mop of sandy hair appeared, and beneath the tumbled hair she saw a cheeky snub-nosed face. Bright wicked eyes gave her no more than a passing glance, as the diminutive figure wriggled to its feet. All its attention was on a heaving mass still imprisoned under the blanket.

'Come on! That's only the tunnel!' the little boy shrieked. 'You've still got to climb the mountains.' He pointed at a perilous pile of dining room chairs.

Another head emerged now from the blanket tunnel. 'Mercy, young Captain!' Beryl squealed as she wriggled into view. Then she saw Virginia and collapsed in helpless laughter on the floor.

Virginia thought she had never seen Beryl look so happy.

'I'm not happy at all, really,' Beryl told her two hours later. 'Quite the reverse. I'm sad—very sad. And worried.'

It was now nine o'clock and she and Virginia were in the kitchen making supper. Frank was upstairs telling a story to young Crispin, who had been put to bed in the spare room.

'His mother just wasn't there when we landed. We telephoned her home, we telephoned her office. We even telephoned your Dr Willoughby.'

'He's not my Dr Willoughby,' corrected Virginia.

'Well, whosoever's—we phoned him. He wasn't there either, so what else could I do but bring Crispin home?'

'Nothing. At least, I can't think of anything else.'

'And neither could I. Neither could the Ops Officer, nor Ken.' Beryl beat up the mashed potatoes with vigour. 'Can you imagine any mother not turning up?'

'No, I can't,' said Virginia. 'Though it happens.'

'Especially,' Beryl went on indignantly, 'with a super child like that.'

'Is he a super child?'

'Oh, certainly.'

'Did you have any difficulty with him?'

'Getting him away from his father? A bit, yes. It wrung the old heart-strings, I can tell you. But Crispin had promised, and his father had promised, and between them they managed it. They kept stiff upper lips in the end. It was awful to see.'

Virginia stirred the cheese sauce and asked, 'What was he like—the father?'

'Rather nice—kind face, quite good-looking in a British diplomat sort of way. Very worried, very sad. I have a horrid idea that he's still in love with that naughty wife of his. He told young Crispin to be sure and look after his mother.'

'Oh, dear!' sighed Virginia.

'Well, it's not really oh, dear—at least, it doesn't have to be. I've given this a lot of thought. In fact all the way back in the plane I kept thinking.'

'Of what?'

'Of a possible happy ending.' Beryl paused.

Virginia said, 'I wish *I* could think of one, but I can't. I don't think Peter's ever going to take to

Crispin, or Crispin to him. And even if he did, that still leaves his father alone.'

'Exactly. But that's not the happy ending *I'm* thinking of. I'm thinking of one that makes everybody happy.'

'Is there such a thing?'

'Yes.'

Beryl began to turn the fluffy potatoes into a hot tureen. 'Wouldn't it be marvellous,' she went on, 'if Crispin's parents were reconciled?'

'Yes, of course it would.'

'Then *you* and Dr Willoughby could get back together again,' Beryl beamed over her shoulder.

Virginia shook her head.

'I don't think it would work. In fact, I know it wouldn't work.'

'Why not?'

'Because you can never put the clock back.'

'Perhaps you're right,' Beryl sighed. 'I suppose it's too good to ever happen. Be a dear, will you, and creep upstairs and tell Frank supper's ready. Don't wake Crispin if he's asleep.'

'I won't.'

Virginia tiptoed softly upstairs and listened outside the spare room door. No sound came from within. She pushed the door open wider.

Crispin lay curled up asleep, his hand still resting inside Frank's. Frank himself was asleep, his chin sunk on his chest, a curious tender expression on his face. Virginia stood looking at them both for several seconds. It was at that moment that *her* idea for a happy ending was suddenly born, though not for herself or even Peter. But for Beryl.

CHAPTER EIGHT

IT was an idea that needed further thought, so Virginia sensibly put it to the back of her mind until she had time to give it that thought. It was her day off the following day. It dawned bright and still, with just a hint of autumn, and she had been planning to go up to London to look at the new autumn clothes in the Oxford Street stores. She had seen a very attractive deep blue suit and matching sweater.

But at breakfast, Crispin put an end to any ideas of shopping. As he dipped his spoon into his bowl of cornflakes, he casually let slip the fact that his mother had promised to take him to Jevington Zoo, before he went back to school—today, in fact.

But now Crispin's announcement had an electrifying and instantaneous effect on both Beryl and Frank. They showed signs of quite disproportionate distress. The tears that welled up in Crispin's knowledgeable eyes were quite unnecessary. So was his wearing of the white airline disc with its message staring the three adults reproachfully in the face: UNACCOMPANIED. PLEASE HELP.

'If only I'd known, son,' said Frank, creasing his brows, 'I'd have asked for the afternoon off and taken you myself. I'm rather partial to zoos— haven't been for donkey's years. It wouldn't have been the same as your mum, of course, but it'd have been better than not going at all.'

Crispin gave him a misty and dismissing little smile and wasted no more time with him. He swivelled his eyes expectantly towards Beryl, and stared at her breathlessly.

Beryl's nice hazel eyes filled with apologetic tears. 'Darling, I *can't!* I'm so sorry, but I'm on standby. Now there's no need to look so cross, Frank! *I* can't help it. I don't do the roster, and rules are rules. A job's a job.'

'Oh, damn your job!' exclaimed Frank with a quite unusual show of temper. 'It's all you ever think of!' He pushed back his chair with such force that it almost fell over.

'That's it!' Beryl replied. 'Now you've said it —what I always suspected. You resent my job, don't you? You want me to stay meekly at home and do nothing.'

A first-class row seemed about to break. Virginia looked in mounting concern from one to the other, trying to convey at least to Beryl her fear of what harm a row between them might do to Crispin.

She need not have worried. She became aware of being stared at by him with an almost hypnotic intensity. She turned her eyes, and met Crispin's unswerving gaze. He ignored the other two, seeming totally unaware of the angry exchanges between the Bests, and was looking at Virginia with the fixed demanding expression of a hungry hound about to be thrown a bone.

'I shall take Crispin,' Virginia announced. 'It's ages since *I've* been to a zoo. I believe it's quite easy to get there, and I'd like to go.'

Crispin thanked her prettily and helped himself to some more cornflakes.

'I really wish I could come as well,' whispered Beryl, as Frank, out of earshot, shouldered his way into his mackintosh. 'But even if I wasn't on stand-by, I really would have to stay here in case Crispin's mother phones, as she's sure to.'

'I don't think so,' Crispin said cheerfully, digging in with his spoon. 'Mother often doesn't turn up. Sometimes she forgets to get me from school. Mother is an artist,' he went on solemnly as if repeating something he had learned by heart. 'They can't be tied down to a time.'

'I see,' Beryl said very disapprovingly. '*That's* what being an artist means, is it?'

Crispin nodded vigorously.

'Mrs Villiers,' Virginia put in, 'designs very beautiful clothes.'

'That's no exc . . .' Beryl began to say, then caught Frank's reproving shake of his head and, to Virginia's surprise, pursed her lips and said nothing.

'She's pretty too,' Crispin smiled proudly. 'Father has a big picture of her in his flat and another in his office, and everyone admires her.' And in the same breath, 'Can I stay here till she comes?'

It was Frank, who seemed to be taking an inordinate time to leave that morning, who replied. 'Of course you can, son! Just as long as you want. And now I must love you and leave you.' He rumpled the boy's hair, then gripped his right hand, and there was the crackle of notes being discreetly passed. 'Expensive places, zoos,' Frank explained.

'There's a fun-fair there as well. You'll need to have a go on everything.'

Crispin seemed reluctant to see Frank depart. 'And will you tell me some more stories, sir? About when you were shipwrecked?'

'Shipwrecked? Frank? He's never been farther than Bognor . . .' Beryl began, then appeared to think better of it.

'Of course I will, lad. Just as soon as I get home.'

'We'll expect you when we see you,' Beryl couldn't resist saying tartly.

'But when will that be?' wailed Crispin. 'When Mother says that it's often *days . . . weeks!*'

'Not a minute later than five o'clock, son. Cross my heart. Just about the time you get back from Jevington Zoo.'

'Aren't you working late tonight, then?' asked Beryl.

'No, no, I've got rid of most of the backlog. No more overtime for a little while.'

'No staff meeting?'

Frank ignored Beryl's sarcasm, shook his head and marched towards the door. 'Staff meeting was last week,' he corrected gently. 'They're only held once a month, Beryl dear.'

'It's amazing,' Beryl remarked drily, as the door closed behind him, 'how Frank can get home on time when he wants to.'

Virginia had already noticed that very obvious fact. It gave credence to the idea she had conceived last night. But she said nothing. She simply allowed Crispin to put his hand on her arm and lead her impatiently away from the breakfast table.

*   *   *

Crispin continued to lead all that day. At six years old, he displayed the outward sophistication of a child too frequently with adults, and warring adults at that. He had learned to play one off against the other and weave through most circumstances to get his own way. Yet beneath the surface, he was vulnerable, endearing and compassionate. Virginia found herself falling under his spell.

He helped Beryl to cut sandwiches for their picnic lunch. He scraped carrots for any donkeys there might be and packed a large bag of buns for the elephants.

He chose to go by the Green Line bus which passed the end of the Ridgeway, rather than by Virginia's car, because he had never been by Green Line before; in London they went everywhere by car or taxi.

They caught the early bus, and managed to get the seat immediately behind the driver. Crispin alternated between driving the bus with the picnic box, and exclaiming at the herds of cows and flocks of sheep and grazing horses visible beyond the hedges.

They were deposited outside the zoo just as the big iron gates were being swung back, and the gatekeeper shook Crispin's hand as the first customer over the threshold, an honour which caused him great jubilation.

A small railway took them round leafy glades where deer and antelope wandered wild. They descended to an aquarium seemingly in a huge black cave where fish could be viewed eyeball to eyeball.

Crispin was enchanted. He seemed determined

to visit every living creature. He held a long conversation with the minah birds, spent a rapt five minutes stroking a giant white rabbit in the Children's Corner, his cheeky snub-nosed face transformed into that of a Botticelli cherub. He wept over a sad little mongoose lying pathetically in a corner of its cage. He gazed in rapt respectful admiration at the polar bears, worried that the lions seemed restless and unhappy, and spent a fortune on nuts for the monkeys.

The monkeys reminded him that he himself felt hungry, so they picked a pleasant spot to eat their lunch, not far from the parrot house, and by the lake. They found a seat under the shade of a willow tree, and he sat on the wooden seat contentedly swinging his legs and feeding the crumbs to a flock of sparrows. The ducks, he had decided, looked well fed enough.

There was one particular undersized sparrow that didn't seem to be getting its share. Crispin did a lot of careful throwing, trying to get the crumbs near to it. Perhaps he identifies with it, Virginia thought sadly. Aloud, she asked, 'Which animal did you like best?'

'I liked them all,' he beamed.

'Even the crocodiles?'

'Yes.'

'And the wolves?'

'I felt sorry for them.'

'Yes, they did look rather bedraggled, didn't they?' Virginia agreed. 'How about the snakes?'

'They were all right. I don't mind snakes.'

'What about the hippo? He didn't seem very friendly.'

'He was shy,' explained Crispin.

'I didn't think animals could be shy.'

'Oh yes, they often are.'

'And the ant-eater?'

'He was funny. I liked him.'

'And the warthogs?'

'Yes, I liked them.'

'Isn't there any animal you don't like?' Virginia put her arm round his thin little shoulders and hugged him.

The smile faded from Crispin's face, to be replaced by the fearful scowl.

'Now what's that frown in aid of?' Virginia teased him. But he thrust out his lower lip and didn't answer. Instead he said at last, 'My teacher says *we're* animals. People are animals.'

'Animals,' Virginia agreed, nodding sagely. 'Yes, of course we are. But special animals.'

The lower lip thrust out further. 'Then there is one animal I don't like,' Crispin said darkly. 'Man.'

'Not all men!' exclaimed Virginia. 'Not your father! Not Frank. Nor the nice man on the gate.'

'No!' Crispin exclaimed hoarsely. 'Of course not!' He made a snuffly noise that was half a sob and half a cry of intolerable anger. 'A man I don't like.'

Virginia didn't ask who.

But Crispin, once launched, was not easily to be stopped. 'He's called . . .'

Gently, Virginia put a finger on his lips. 'Don't say it, Crispin. Don't even think it. You don't really know him yet. He's probably very nice. You'll get to like him one day . . .'

Then she realised that Crispin wasn't listening to

her. His sharp intelligent eyes were fixed on a group of three people on the other side of the lake.

'There's Mother!' he yelped, jumping to his feet, and waving his arms wildly. 'Mother! She's come! I knew she would. I knew she'd want to see me. She got the wrong day, that's all!' He jumped up and down in excitement, then shaded his eyes.

Then abruptly, the excitement faded and he slumped back on the seat in an attitude of complete deflation and abandonment. 'Oh, no, no!' He flung his arms across his chest and buried his head in them. He began to sob. Through the sobs, eventually came the muffled words, 'She's got *him*.'

'Him, Crispin?'

'Him—him. She's got him with her, the one you asked me about. The one I don't like. *Him*—Dr Willoughby!'

Virginia sat stroking the boy's heaving shoulders for a moment or two. When, at last, as his sobs quietened, she turned to look over her shoulder, she saw that things were worse even than she had realised. She and Crispin had been spotted by the little party, who were coming round the lake towards them—first a woman, hurrying and waving, then Peter Willoughby, his fair hair unmistakable. Then, to her horror, she saw that the third person in the party was not, as she had at first supposed, the driver of Mrs Villiers' car, but Richard Tranter himself.

A scene which was to haunt Virginia for nights afterwards then took place. For ever afterwards, she thought, when I smell lake water and hear the sound of ducks and geese, I shall remember the tearful reunion between Crispin and his mother, and Crispin's furious rejection of Peter. But most of all she knew she would remember Richard Tranter's blazing blue eyes fixed on her, and the expression of his mouth curled in contempt.

Standing by, as helpless as Peter, Virginia listened as Mrs Villiers told Crispin what had happened. She had mistaken the date. He knew Mummy—she often did. She had had to design an important gown for an important client—she whispered in his ear just how important—and the worry and rush and the artistry that had been required had quite muddled the date in her mind. Dr Willoughby and she had come down by train today, to find *no* Crispin. She had quite thought his heartless father had kept him from her again. Well, he'd done it once, he could do it twice. It was all too much to bear, and she had understandably collapsed, fallen in a faint there in Arrivals. Dr Willoughby had taken her to the medical section to recover, and Dr Tranter, such a charming man, had been *so* kind. He had found out that Crispin had spent the night at the Bests', and that for some reason Sister Mayhew had decided to bring him to the zoo.

So here they were. All was well now. Dr Tranter was going to take them to the station in his car, and they would get the train back to London. Crispin loved trains, didn't he? And they would go to Harrods for tea, buttered muffins and cream cakes, and afterwards Dr Willoughby was going to take him to the toy department. What could be nicer?

With trepidation, Virginia saw the terrible scowl return to Crispin's face. He thrust out his lower lip and said, 'Not with *him!* I'm not going back with him. He doesn't like me, and I don't like him. I don't ever want him to live with us. I told Ginny . . .'

At that point, Virginia became aware that Dr Tranter, by a peremptory jerk of his head, was indicating that she and he should leave the others to argue it out themselves.

At least, that was what she thought was his intention. In fact, when they were out of earshot of the unhappy trio, Virginia realised that his intention was quite different. She was being taken aside for a private castigation.

'Well,' he demanded, resting one foot on a fallen log, and folding his arms across his chest, 'what have you got to say for yourself this time?'

'What have I to say for myself?' she repeated. 'I'm not sure what you mean?'

'Come, come, you're an intelligent young woman.' He paused. 'You know perfectly well what I mean.' He stared down at her, his eyes probing and intense.

Virginia met his eyes coolly at first, then when she could hold his gaze no longer, she said, 'I simply tried to entertain Crispin. His mother had promised to bring him to the zoo, so I brought him instead.'

'I hardly think that was necessary.'

'Not necessary, perhaps. But it seemed to be a good idea at the time.'

Dr Tranter straightened and glanced over his shoulder to where Mrs Villiers and Crispin and Peter were all arguing furiously. 'Does it still seem a good idea?' he asked.

'I think he enjoyed himself for a while.'

'Didn't you think of the effect on Mrs Villiers when she found no Crispin?'

'What about the effect on young Crispin when she didn't turn up yesterday?'

'Most reprehensible,' Dr Tranter conceded. 'But Mrs Villiers now fears you're trying to drive a wedge between Crispin and Dr Willoughby.'

'Drive a wedge?' Virginia exploded. She began to say, 'I could drive a coach and horses,' then something forbidding in Dr Tranter's expression made her stop in mid-sentence. Instead she asked bleakly, 'Did you accept that?'

'Certainly not. I totally rejected such a suggestion.' He shot her a level look. 'You're my staff, I defend you.'

'Thank you,' she said coldly.

'Though naturally I reserve my own private opinion on the matter.'

'And am I to be given that private opinion?'

He raised his brows. 'I think not.'

'But I can guess it!' Virginia exclaimed.

Richard Tranter went on as if she hadn't spoken. 'I shall, however, give you my opinion as your Section Chief.' He paused and said slowly, 'I think that despite your mature approach to your work, you still let your heart rule your head. We need minds uncluttered by emotions—to know how far we can get involved, and when to draw the line.'

'And where, in this instance, should I have drawn the line?'

'You should have kept Crispin in one place till his mother was found, instead of having our medical section cluttered with an hysterical female.'

He frowned over his shoulder at the trio as the sound of their raised voices floated above the quacking of the ducks and the honking of the geese.

'At least I'm sure you never let *your* heart rule your head!' Virginia exclaimed bitterly, watching his expression.

He inclined his head as if acknowledging a compliment. 'I try not to,' he said modestly.

Thinking about it afterwards, Virginia decided he had probably made that remark in self-parody. But she was in no mood to appreciate subtlety of voice or expression. Angrily she remarked, 'It would make you more human if you didn't try so hard!'

For a second he looked astonished, even faintly amused at her outburst, then he said something about finding it all too easy to be human. He was obviously thinking of Clare, for momentarily his mouth softened. But only momentarily. Crispin had begun to shout words no six-year-old should know.

'I suggest we rejoin the others,' Dr Tranter said drily, putting his hand under Virginia's elbow to turn her round.

Perhaps because of their antagonism, she felt herself disturbingly aware of the touch of his fingers. She was glad when he released her almost at once, and they walked the few steps back to the others in silence.

They were in a state of considerable turmoil. Mrs Villiers was crying now, the mascara running down her cheeks in ugly smudges, while Peter was running his hand through his hair in the last stages of exasperation.

Crispin held the centre of the stage. 'Just let *us* go, Mother. Not him. I won't go with him, not even if you carry me!' He stamped his feet and kicked out towards Peter Willoughby's shins. 'Never, never, nev . . .'

The third 'never' simply died away as Richard Tranter unhurriedly and effortlessly seized him and flung him over his shoulder fireman fashion. 'We'll soon see about that,' he said evenly, and when Crispin began to kick he gave him a not ungentle smack on the seat of his pants, which reduced Crispin to appalled and astonished silence.

'Come along, Mrs Villiers . . . Willoughby,' and Richard began to march off towards the exit. He didn't bother to summon Virginia by name; he seemed to take it for granted that she would follow, like an Arab wife.

Reaching the car park, and his car, he addressed her carelessly. He freed a hand, dipped it in his jacket pocket and handed her the car keys. 'Open it up, please. Take the catch off the back seat door. This young brat's going to sit in the back till he learns to behave himself.' He deposited Crispin quite gently but firmly on the upholstery. Then he turned to Peter. 'You get in with him.'

'I think it's best really,' Mrs Villiers protested uncertainly, 'if Peter follows on later.'

'I agree,' Peter mopped his brow. 'I feel wrung out, exhausted. All in all, I've had enough for one day!'

'Suit yourselves.' Richard Tranter looked from one to the other. 'This is entirely your affair. But in my opinion, you should start as you mean to go on. Be firm. Give in now, and you'll go on giving in.'

From the back seat, Crispin's bright eyes watched them in well-behaved silence. But he knew he'd won. As his mother climbed into the back seat to sit beside him, he took her hand and squeezed. But it was on Richard Tranter that his admiring gaze rested.

'I'm beginning to think it's Fate,' said Peter, as Richard's car swept away leaving them both standing side by side at the zoo exit. 'You were so right when you said not to rush into marriage.'

'Did you tell your fiancée I said that?' asked Virginia.

'Well, I had to—I mean, I had to say that I'd taken the advice of an old friend. After all, we're having to postpone the marriage, for a while. One has to give a reason.'

'Doesn't she think it is a good thing, to postpone?'

'Oh, all in all, yes. We've got to get Crispin sorted out. That's our number one priority—get him off our backs, get him into a good boarding school.'

'He's a bit young,' she protested.

'He's old in his ways—clever little devil, cunning, as you saw. What he needs is a good old-fashioned boarding school.'

Virginia said nothing. Automatically, she had begun to turn her steps towards the bus stop. She was not sure what to do about Peter, nor what her attitude should be. She had not yet digested the traumatic events of the last half hour.

When the bus arrived she clambered aboard. Peter followed her. 'I can't do less than see you home,' he said gallantly, and paid her fare. 'It certainly was a turn-up for the book, wasn't it? Though not altogether unexpected. I suppose I should be firmer with the monster. But if I'd tried doing what Tranter did, the little devil would have gouged my eyes out.'

'Dr Tranter has a habit of getting away with things,' Virginia said, astonished to hear a note of admiration creep into her voice.

'He always was a high-handed devil. Can't think how you put up with him.' And in the same breath, 'How about us going out for dinner tonight? Entwick Manor again?'

'I think I'd better not. Beryl will be organising dinner.'

'Would she mind if I shared a bite?'

'I'm sure she wouldn't.'

Virginia fell into another silence. For the first time she began to think of how Beryl and Frank would take Crispin's unceremonious departure.

Beryl actually came running to the front window of the lounge as Virginia let the gate click shut behind them. Virginia glimpsed her anxious face through the window and then the front door was flung open.

Virginia effected introductions. 'I'm delighted to meet you at last,' Beryl said to Peter. 'Ginny here has spoken so much of you. You'll stay for supper, won't you? I've got plenty. We thought, you see, that Crispin might still be here.' Determinedly, she smiled brightly. 'But he isn't. And his mother turned up, and that's a very good thing. I'm glad she found you.'

'Did Dr Tranter come here?' asked Virginia,

casually taking off her coat.

'No, he phoned. He didn't say much—brusque and to the point, as usual. I told him you'd taken Crispin to the zoo, and he said, "That figures".'

'What did he mean by that?'

Beryl shrugged. 'I don't know. I suppose he meant it was in your character—typically you. Anyway, all's well that ends well. Was Crispin delighted to see his mother?'

'Very.'

'All smiles then, I bet.'

'Not altogether,' Peter said with charming ruefulness. 'He wasn't pleased to see me.'

'I can't think why,' Beryl smiled warmly, and bustled into the kitchen to make the inevitable tea. When she returned with the pot and some pink iced cakes, she continued, 'But Crispin's a lovely lad underneath.'

'How far underneath?' asked Peter.

'Not far. Frank and I really took to him.' A thought struck her. 'Frank's going to be ever so disappointed he isn't here.' For once when she spoke of Frank, her mouth became tender and concerned. She began looking at the clock again.

She didn't look for long. At ten to five, they heard the click of the gate, followed by the sound of Frank's key in the door. Then there was a considerable lapse of time, while Beryl looked anxious and Peter looked mildly surprised but continued to help himself to the excellent iced cakes.

Finally, there came a rustling of paper, then the door was kicked open to allow Frank to come in carrying a large parcel in either hand. 'Well, son? Which hand do you take first?'

Red-faced and beaming with anticipatory pleasure, he looked round the room. 'Come out, young
rascal! Wherever you are! I know you're hiding.'
He padded over to the sofa and peered behind it.
Then he became aware of Peter, and of Beryl rising
to her feet to come over and put her arms round
him.

'He's gone, lovie, Crispin's gone. His mother
came for him. Isn't that nice?'

Then as he let the parcels slide to the floor she
buried her head in his chest and began to weep.

CHAPTER NINE

'THEY were tears of happiness, of course,' Beryl said over supper. 'It was a happy ending, and I like happy endings.' Still intent on happy endings, she looked across the table at Frank, and said meaningfully, 'I thought you and I might go out later on this evening. There's a good film on in Grantly—a reissue of *Love Story*. And this young couple could stay in and have the place cosily to themselves.'

It seemed churlish, Virginia thought, to point out that they were not a young couple, and that anyway she didn't want to have the house to herself with Peter. At least, she supposed she didn't. Certainly she oughtn't to if she did, and that was almost the same thing.

Frank agreed with the eager enthusiasm of a black sheep suddenly and unexpectedly invited into the fold. 'Yes. It's ages since we've been to a film. I'd like that.'

'Oughtn't you to be getting back to London?' Virginia asked Peter. 'Didn't you say you'd follow Mrs Villiers on a later train?'

'Oh, let them have the evening to themselves—mother and son,' Peter waved his hand magnanimously.

'You don't want to turn out now, Peter,' Beryl agreed. 'It's raining cats and dogs. Stay the night. Crispin's room is all ready.'

'If you promise it isn't haunted by him,' Peter

smiled, and Beryl laughed. Clearly she found him as charming as he intended her to find him.

'If it is,' she smiled, 'it's a very nice ghost.' She began piling the supper dishes on to a tray.

'Leave all that,' Virginia told her. 'Go and change—put on that new dress. Peter and I'll do the washing up.'

When Beryl appeared twenty minutes later, in a new dark green woollen dress and high-heeled matching shoes, Peter and she had almost finished.

'My, my,' Beryl laughed, swirling around to show off her dress, 'you look a proper married couple! You never told me Peter was so domesticated. I thought he was just a handsome face.'

Peter bowed, murmured that she looked divine and admitted he was a man of many hidden accomplishments.

One of those accomplishments was undoubtedly making a woman feel that he loved her. Virginia doubted if any woman could forget that. Lest she had, Peter seemed set on reminding her. When the dishes had been put away, and Frank and Beryl waved off to the cinema, Peter pushed the big velvet sofa in front of the fire. Then he sorted through Frank's cassettes, and chose a selection from the Beatles. He built up the fire, turned out the lights, and drew Virginia down on to the sofa beside him.

The haunting strains of 'Yesterday, All my troubles seemed so far away . . .' filled the shadowy room. He slipped his arm round her shoulders and pulled her to him so that her head was resting against his chest. He made no attempt to kiss her. They simply stared into the flickering firelight, while the music seemed to say everything that he wanted it to. And for a while, everything *she* wanted it to. She felt a moment of almost unbearable sweetness and longing.

When finally, unhurriedly, he tilted up her chin with his free hand, and tantalisingly brushed her lips with his, she was ready to be kissed. Her lips parted, and about to return his kiss, she opened her eyes. She saw his gazing down at her, heavy with desire, and thought as clearly as if a balloon had appeared above her head, 'But not by him.'

She suddenly realised she had been wistfully dreaming, but not of him—but she refused to admit to herself who had filled her mind. Firmly she disentangled herself. 'I'll go and make some coffee,' she said, and tried to get to her feet.

'No, don't! I don't want anything. I just want to sit here with you, like we used to.'

'A lot has happened since then,' she said quietly. 'And you're engaged to someone else.'

'Oh, I know—*I know!* Don't remind me! I've been stupid.' Unable to recapture her hand, Peter sat forward with his elbows on his knees, holding his head in his hands in an attitude of despair.

In the silence, a piece of blazing coal fell from the fire on to the hearth and died to a cinder, sending off a faint whiff of smoke that stung her eyes. Like their love, Virginia thought sadly.

When Peter's attitude of despair failed to rouse her, he dropped his hands to his knees and turning to her asked in a desperate tone, 'What *am* I to do, Ginny?'

'About Crispin?'

'No, not just about him, but about the whole

damned business. About marrying Antonia. She's quite a handful, too, you know—not the sort of wife for an up-and-coming man. I'm not at all sure I can cope.'

Virginia thought for a moment, then said slowly, 'I'm not the best person to advise you.'

He pounced on her hand and held it to his breast. 'Because you're still in love with me yourself?' he asked in such a theatrical tone of voice that she actually laughed out loud.

It made it somehow easier to say, 'No, Peter, because I'm *not!*' The words slipped out before she was aware of her intention to say them. Certainly before she realised their uncompromising truthfulness.

'Not in love with me?'

'No.'

'But you were once!' he protested indignantly.

'No,' she corrected, 'I *thought* I was once.'

'And what has effected this sudden revelation?' he asked, scowling. 'How do you *know* you're not?'

She shrugged. She wondered sadly how it was possible to explain to Peter that it was like watching a candle flame die in the sudden light of the sun. 'I'll also tell you something else,' she said instead. '*You* weren't in love with *me* either. And I doubt if you've ever been in love. Otherwise you'd cope with Crispin, believe me. And you wouldn't mind if Antonia *is* a handful. Or if she'd make a good wife for an ambitious man.'

She had expected Peter to take exception to her remarks, and to challenge her as to how she knew so much about love now. But instead he jumped up and taking hold of both her hands, pulled her to her feet. He beamed as if with relief. He looked ten years younger, an unsophisticated young house-man again. 'Dear Ginny,' he said, kissing her in a brotherly fashion on her forehead. 'Trust you to straighten things out! You always could.' He hug-ged her to him. 'You've taken a weight off my mind. I see things so much clearer now. Come on,' he pulled her over to the cassette player, 'let's celebrate. Let's dance. Beryl won't mind if we roll back these rugs, will she?'

Without waiting for Virginia to reply he pushed the sofa out of the way and rolled up the rugs. 'Now what shall we start on? Frank's got quite a collec-tion. A sentimental chap at heart, I'd say, old Frank. How about a tango? We always cut a dash with a tango, I remember. Do you remember that time we won the prize? And do you remember Matron doing the paso doble with the Chairman of the Governors, and falling over his feet?'

Suddenly their roles to one another had changed. They were young again and they were friends, and the past changed to something painless and precious.

'I hope the neighbours are deaf,' Peter laughed as the cassette played 'Jealousy', and he swung her round the small floor with his old skill.

'They're away!' Virginia shouted above the music.

'Thank heaven for that.' He began singing the words: 'The heartaches I cost you, no wonder I lost you.' But he sang them in high spirits, not trying to say anything to her, except perhaps that he was pleased they were still friends.

So relaxed had they both become with one

another, and so loud was the music, that at first they hardly heard the outraged knocking on the front door.

When they did, Peter turned up his eyes to the ceiling. 'Uh, uh,' he groaned, 'who said the neighbours were away? Famous last words!' Still holding her firmly round the waist, he swirled her out into the hall. 'Humble apologies called for,' he whispered, and with his free hand pulled back the catch of the front door and flung it back. 'I do most humbly apologise, for our little celebration . . .' he began, when his voice died away to a groan.

Tall and grim-faced in the spotlight of the porch lamp stood Richard Tranter. Slowly, his eyes travelled from one to the other, taking in, no doubt, their dishevelled appearance, their bright eyes and the fact that they were so manifestly enjoying themselves.

'I have a letter for the Bests,' he announced curtly after what seemed an age of disapproving silence, 'from young Crispin. I promised I would deliver it.'

'That's very kind of you, sir!' Peter exclaimed with the effusiveness of guilt.

'Not at all. Your fiancée was most grateful for their kindness.' At the words 'your fiancée' Peter's guilty nervousness increased. His hand still clasped Virginia's waist as if he had forgotten about it. But seeing Richard Tranter's eyes fixed steadily in that direction, he dropped it like a hot coal.

'Won't you come in, Doctor?' Virginia invited, recalling herself.

He shook his head. 'Thank you, no.' He transferred his gaze to Peter. 'And talking of your fiancée, I suggest you phone her. She won't know where you are and she may be worried. I take it you are spending the night here?'

'I'll get on to her right away—I was going to, but time flies.'

Richard Tranter made some biting remark about time flying when one is enjoying oneself, and said good night. With relief Peter closed the door.

'Phew!' he exclaimed, leaning against the panels and mopping his brow, 'what a high-handed, imperious devil he is! Pity the girl that falls in love with *him*!'

'I do,' Virginia said fervently. 'I pity her with all my heart.'

CHAPTER TEN

PETER left Number Seven early the next morning. He had a full list of appointments, and he seemed anxious now, after the encounter with Dr Tranter, to be gone. He gave both Beryl and Virginia a peck on the cheek. Frank was to drop him off at the station.

'Well, *you* don't seem to have made use of your opportunity,' Beryl sighed, clearing away the breakfast things. 'I tried to throw you together. He obviously wanted to make it up to you, or why did he come back here?'

'A number of reasons.' Virginia pushed back her chair. 'I don't think he really knows what he wants.'

'Men rarely do,' murmured Beryl, but without asperity. 'But I'd say Peter knows better than most.'

Virginia changed the subject. 'Did you enjoy the film?'

'Very much. It's a lovely film, very romantic. It was like old times. We actually held hands! Oh, by the way, did you see Crispin's letter?'

'Yes, Frank showed it to me.'

The letter had been brief and showed no great handwriting aptitude, but Frank and Beryl had exclaimed over it as if it were the work of an infant prodigy. It said merely, in an ill-formed jumble of small letters and capitals, 'Thank you for having me. Can I come again?'

'Frank was as pleased as a dog with two tails,' Beryl added.

'So I saw.' Virginia put on her cloak. Her mind was now on the day ahead. How was she going to face Dr Tranter? And what would he have to say?

Happily, she was spared finding out, at least for that day.

Rosie greeted her as she came into the Medical Section with the information that the Chief was about to fly to Zambia, where the crew of an outgoing service there had gone down with a mysterious illness.

'Oh, dear,' Virginia stopped in her tracks. 'Nothing dangerous, I hope?'

'Haven't a clue, Sister. Could be anything out there. It was all a bit above my head.'

Sister Porter was hardly more informative. The telex had come in round about six a.m. She'd called out Dr Tranter and he'd come round straight away. He was due to take off shortly. He was just collecting what he needed. He was taking vaccines for such diseases where they would be appropriate, and Malaprin and Promazin . . . but there were so many things it could be . . . there were some diseases you just had to hope and pray it wasn't.

She looked worried. Her husband had to hoot his horn twice before she exclaimed, 'Hubby's here!' and took her leave.

Immediately she had gone, Virginia left her office, crossed the treatments room, and knocked on the Chief's door. She turned the handle as his exasperated voice said crisply, 'Come in if you must.'

He had his back to the door and was just pushing

his stethoscope into a bulging zipbag. He added, without turning, 'See Sister about whatever it is —I'm on my way to Departures.'

'I know,' she said softly. 'I was wondering if I might volunteer to come too.'

He spun round at the sound of her voice. His face seemed momentarily exposed and naked and vulnerable, and his eyes were shadowed. Just for a second, she glimpsed something very like tenderness, then the cool efficient mask came down. 'Certainly not, Sister. You're needed to hold the fort here.' He gave a fierce jerk to the zip and succeeded in pulling it shut. He made to pass her, and she put her hand on his arm without realising she had done so. 'Don't take too many risks,' she said, removing her hand.

He looked down at her mockingly for a moment, 'Don't let my heart rule my head?' he raised his brows. 'Hardly likely.' He patted her shoulder dismissingly and was gone.

Almost at once the phone rang, and the day's work began. The first patient was in the passenger terminal. A little girl passenger running excitedly down the stairs had fallen, both hands outstretched.

'They'd just returned from Majorca, poor lass,' the traffic girl said, 'but at least I suppose it's better than happening when you're just setting out.'

'I'll be along right away.' Virginia seized her bag and then took the precaution of summoning the ambulance, and hurried up the Cord. Within twelve minutes, the child had been despatched to the County Hospital with her parents in attendance, and within thirty-five, Virginia was entering in the book, *suspected fracture of both wrists*.

Poor child, she thought for a moment, her pen poised. She had been only a couple of years older than Crispin. But then perhaps she wasn't so poor after all—both parents were there, both concerned and supportive, a happy, united little trio. From Crispin, her mind strayed again to Richard Tranter.

Through her office window she had only intermittent glimpses of the runways. She could hear the aircraft taking off, but only glimpse them distantly, in that unfilled wedge between the hangars. Nevertheless, her eyes kept straying to it, as if from that glimpse she might identify the aircraft that was taking him away, and wish him well.

Before ten o'clock a queue of people began to form outside her door for injections—a group of four oil rig men who had forgotten or just hadn't bothered to have their cholera injections, a married couple travelling to Malaysia who'd left their antimalarial tablets behind, and a business man travelling to West Africa who needed a yellow fever jab. Africa sparked off in her mind her worries about Dr Tranter. A list of diseases painful and dangerous came unbidden into her mind, but she refused to dwell on them.

The day spun by. She was summoned again to the terminal, this time to treat a man with what she was certain was a perforated gastric ulcer. She had scarcely time to enter PGU in the diagnosis column, having whisked him away stat to the County Hospital, when a van driver was brought in with a cut head after skidding into a bollard. A workman with an electric burn on his hand and forearm followed him, then came a schoolboy with a tooth abscess and a dear old gentleman who had angina pains.

Sister Mortimer arrived on her moped before Virginia realised that she had had no lunch and it was already time to go home. The sky was becoming dark and stormy, but a cheerful fire was burning in Number Seven when she arrived. Scarcely had Virginia showered and changed into a pair of slacks and a sweater than Beryl was calling up that supper was ready and Frank had promised to come home early.

The three of them ate a companionable meal. Beryl's attitude towards Frank appeared softer. She was going out on duty the following morning to take a party of schoolchildren to Edinburgh, and she volunteered to bring him some shortbread. After supper was cleared away, they announced their intention of composing a letter to Crispin. Frank had decided, apparently, to write out the story he would have told Crispin had he reappeared.

'The one about your shipwrick?' Beryl asked, only this time quite without sarcasm. Indeed with respect.

'That's right,' Frank said cheerfully, 'in my days before the mast. He likes that sort of adventure stuff—most kids do. You can help me if you like.'

Companionably, they put their heads together. Only one thing marred the happy convivial evening. When the story was finished, Frank suggested it would be a lot easier for Crispin to read if he got his typist at the office to type it out.

Beryl's face suddenly changed. 'I don't want to

bring your typist into this,' she said huffily. 'She'd probably laugh at it. And no doubt she's got quite enough to do, with all your overtime.'

'Oh, she won't mind. She's a nice lass, she'll enjoy it. She's just a kid herself—she only left school last winter.'

It gave Virginia more food for thought. She lay awake a long time that night, thinking hard. The idea she had conceived for Beryl gained strength.

Though Virginia's own love life was in ruins and she found the greatest difficulty in interpreting her own heart, she seemed to have acquired a peculiar insight into that of her friend. If anyone had told Virginia that such insight was often the perquisite of someone in love, she would have firmly dismissed that idea. She was not in love with anyone now. Peter had lost his old magic for her, and there was no one whom she dared allow to take his place.

But, when she fell asleep, she dreamed that night of Richard Tranter. It was a nightmare in which he was in some jungle swamp menaced by tsetse flies and mosquitoes and malaria and blackwater fever and encephalitis. The reality was no doubt quite the opposite, she told herself; Dr Tranter was probably staying at some smart new hotel in the Zambian capital, having discovered the crew were suffering from nothing more serious than a mild attack of 'flu.

Nevertheless, she was unusually silent over breakfast, aware somehow of the fragility of love and life. Frank left early in cheerful spirits. A picture postcard had arrived from Crispin that morning. It showed a picture of the *Arethusa*, and in the awful capitals and small letters it asked, 'Is this like your ship?'

'Frank's quite given his heart to that child,' Beryl remarked as the door closed behind him. She slipped on the jacket of her smart brown and gold uniform, and looked at herself critically in the oval mirror over the fireplace. 'I'm lucky,' she went on, 'I see a lot of children—too many, sometimes.'

Virginia resolved that the time had come to put her idea into practice. 'Doesn't something strike you, Beryl?' she asked.

'No.' Beryl turned to regard her. 'Not specially. Why?'

'Something that might be wrong between you and Frank.'

'I don't want to talk about that. Anyway, I know what's wrong.'

'What?'

'His typist. Even last night, I saw that—the way his face softened when he spoke about her. You must have seen it too.'

'But she's only a kid!' protested Virginia.

'So?'

'So?'

'So, Frank loves young people. He's good with them. He's a real family man. So are you—a family woman.' Virginia drew a deep breath. 'Hasn't it ever struck you that it's high time you stopped looking after other people's children, and started staying at home and having children of your own?'

Aware of Beryl's outraged intake of breath, she rose and put on her cloak. Beryl seemed to have been struck speechless.

But she found her voice as Virginia put her hand on the latch. 'And don't you think it's high time you stopped thinking about other people's hang-ups, and started sorting out your own love affair?'

It was the first time that Beryl had been anything but kind. But then she was being cruel to be kind, Virginia thought, as she drove to the airport. Beryl was perfectly right. As her grandmother used to say, there's only one person you can do anything about, and that's yourself. Unfortunately loving always meant involving another person, and there was precious little you could do about that.

When she arrived at the medical section she looked hopefully for Dr Tranter's bicycle, but neither his nor Miss Todd's was there. Rosie, divining her mind, called out, 'The Chief's airborne at the moment, somewhere between Zambia and here. Looks like he's sorted out whatever had to be sorted out—Night Sister got a telex.'

The telex merely gave his time of arrival, and the fact that no action would be needed by the Port Health Authority. Which meant, at least, that it had been nothing infectious. Virginia's spirits rose.

Then Clare Todd arrived in a smart convertible, and Virginia heard her informing Rosie that the Chief had phoned her last night at her flat, all the way from Zambia. He was going straight back to his place, after he landed to catch up on his sleep. She would leave early to prepare him a meal.

The day sped by. At one o'clock, while she was strapping a passenger's sprained ankle, Rosie came in with a box of sandwiches. 'I thought you looked peaky this morning, Sister,' she said, 'and I bet you wouldn't say no to one of these. The Chief's aircraft's in the circuit. Clare's gone to meet him in.'

Virginia didn't see him till the following morning. He was already in the section, dictating a memorandum on his dictaphone to go out to all aircrew on eating suspect food and the dangers of salmonella poisoning.

'Come in, Sister,' when she knocked in answer to the red flashing light. 'You should listen to this —something for you to learn to keep an eye on.' He waved her to a chair, and she folded her hands in her lap, lowered her eyes and listened meekly. But with difficulty. She found it hard to reconcile her own contradictory mood in which a lightness of heart that Richard had returned unscathed struggled with her apprehension that he would now refer to finding Peter and her together and would again take the opportunity to reprove her.

If he felt anything of her mood, it didn't seem to affect him. Crisply, he was reminding everyone concerned that it was supposed to be standard practice, for obvious reasons, for the Captain of the aircraft not to be served with the same meal as the crew. This practice had obviously been flouted. So too, had common sense. Any food which tasted unpleasant or might be contaminated should be immediately rejected. It had only been by sheer fortune that a certain crew had brought the aircraft to a safe landing, some time before themselves collapsing.

'Well, let's hope that's a lesson to them,' he said, turning to Virginia and switching off the dictaphone.

She wanted to say how glad she was that he was back. But that was for Clare to do. So instead, she murmured, 'I'm glad it was nothing more serious.'

'It was serious enough,' he frowned. 'They're still in hospital. Now how did you cope while I was away?'

'I coped,' Virginia told him. 'Would you like to see the entries?'

He nodded. 'I'll come through to your office.' He opened the door for her. 'Sit down,' he pulled out her chair for her. 'I'll stand—I've been sitting for too long.' He whistled through his teeth as he leaned over her, his finger travelling down the entries. She watched his finger pause at entry Number 8. 'And *was* it a PGU?' he asked her.

She nodded. 'Yes. I telephoned the hospital that evening. He's doing all right.'

'Good.' Dr Tranter nodded, his eyes on her face. 'Good for you. You've got a flair for diagnosis.'

'Thank you.' She flushed scarlet.

'That's exactly what we need here—a good diagnostician. Calm nerves, a pleasant manner, deft hands, quick feet.'

Quite overwhelmed at this dazzling list of her virtues, Virginia looked up at him, her eyes wide and glowing with pleasure. Her gaze seemed to totally unnerve him, as no defiant gaze of hers had ever done. He cleared his throat uncomfortably, then his tone altered. 'Yes, Sister,' he said gruffly, speaking the next word with heavy emphasis, as if it were to himself as well as her he spoke to, '*professionally*, I have no complaints.'

CHAPTER ELEVEN

VIRGINIA had only a few days to pride herself on that qualified compliment, when that too proved to be what Peter would have called 'Famous last words.' Those days, though, were singularly sweet. She and Richard made a good team. And though she was never completely able to forget her physical awareness of him, she knew she was completely successful in hiding it behind a cool professionalism. She was thankful that he was on duty with her. The day brought a series of serious cases —a passenger suffering a stroke, an airframe worker almost severing his hand, an aircraft arriving in from the Middle East with a passenger in a coma. And simultaneous with the telephone summons for these, a queue of patients with more minor problems, clamouring in the waiting room that they had planes and connections to catch.

By a quarter to four, the waiting room had emptied. Dr Tranter had returned to his office, and Virginia was just about to sign the day's log, when Rosie put her head round the door. 'Another customer, Sister. Traffic's coming up with a walking transit case.'

Almost at once there came the sound of agitated voices from down the corridor. 'Here they are.' Rosie stepped back to allow into the office a Traffic girl holding a tall elderly woman by the arm. The woman wore a beaded headband and long ear-rings. She flung herself into the vacant chair, clapped her hands over her ears and groaned theatrically in a voice with a pronounced French accent, 'I want to die!'

'Madame Lavoisier's just flown in from Sydney,' the Traffic girl explained. 'The aircraft had to make a steep descent, and Madame's ears are paining her.'

'Madame's ears have been ruined,' the passenger stopped groaning to announce. 'And a singer's ears too—*quelle catastrophe!*'

'And the trouble is she's in transit. She's got a connection to Zürich in two hours' time, and she still wants to catch it.'

'She must catch it,' corrected Madame Lavoisier. 'I have a concert to give.' She lapsed into a waterfall of French. From her own schoolgirl French, Virginia gathered that no obstructive person was going to say she couldn't fly on. Nurse must give her an injection immediately and some pills, and Madame would if necessary die on the way.

With difficulty, Virginia coaxed her into the treatment room and examined her ears. With even greater difficulty she tried to explain that she was suffering from Bara-trauma: her eardrums had become inflamed. But the pain would wear off and no harm would be done. Anyway, it would be very unwise to fly on immediately—Madame's eardrums might well perforate if exposed to further damage.

Madame Lavoisier was outraged beyond belief. How dared Nurse be so stupid and obstructive? Concerts didn't grow on trees! She jumped to her feet and was about to storm out, when

Dr Tranter opened the door.

His presence seemed to fill and calm the office. He looked relaxed and kindly. 'Why, Madame Lavoisier!' he said, as if he hadn't heard the noise that had been going on for the last quarter of an hour. 'Our receptionist told me you were here.' He waved her back to her chair and perched himself on the edge of the treatments room table. He extended his hand and shook hers, smiling at her, in admiration—and not feigned admiration either, Virginia noticed. So did Madame Lavoisier. Visibly, she melted.

'I went to your first London concert, Madame. I was enthralled.'

Madame beamed. 'I shall come to London again one day.'

'That *is* good news,' Dr Tranter smiled. 'But first we must do our best to look after such sensitive and valuable ears.'

The battle was over before it had properly begun.

Meekly Madame allowed him to re-examine her. Meekly she accepted the same diagnosis. Meekly she listened to Dr Tranter painstakingly explaining about the function of the Eustachian tube in regulating ear pressure, and the value of rest and allowing time for recovery. She made no demur when Dr Tranter asked the Traffic girl to book Madame into the nearest comfortable hotel—indeed, she apologised.

'I am sorry to be impatient,' Madame explained sadly. 'But as one gets older, one's concert bookings, alas, get less.'

'You have still a great deal to give, Madam,'

Dr Tranter squeezed her thin shoulder reassuringly. 'Take my word for it. You have many, many admirers. Now get some rest, and tomorrow I shall examine your ears again.'

How kind and perceptive he can be, Virginia thought. He has overruled Madame but left her with her dignity intact, her confidence renewed.

'Already, dear Doctor, my ears are improving. The pain is less. But till tomorrow.' Madame Lavoisier blew him a kiss. 'And for my next London concert, you shall have tickets from me. Bring your pretty little nurse.'

When Madame Lavoisier and the Traffic girl had gone, the treatments room seemed quiet and expectant.

Virginia sighed. Dr Tranter had seemed so gentle, approachable and human. She wished she had the courage to say, 'If you admire Madame Lavoisier, then *I'd* like to hear her. I feel I would like the things you like. I'd love to go to the concert with you.' But she couldn't, of course. If Madame did again get a London booking and the tickets came, then naturally it must be Clare who accompanied him.

But the feeling of empathy between them was dangerously sweet. When she found herself wishing Clare Todd wasn't in love with Dr Tranter, Virginia had to force herself to terminate it. Briskly and with unusual noise and vigour, she began to tidy her desk.

Richard watched her for a moment with his eyebrows sardonically raised.

'Shall I make the entry, Doctor?' she asked, unscrewing her pen.

'Please do, Sister,' he nodded to her as he walked back to his office. His eyes were cool again, his mouth hard. The moment had gone.

But it had been, she thought, listening to the putter of Sister Mortimer's bike. It had been.

She returned to Number Seven hugging the memory of it to her. Beryl had not returned from Edinburgh, so Virginia put on the oven and heated the dinner Beryl had left for Frank and herself.

He came in reasonably early, looking quite pleased with himself. His typist had made a good job of typing out the shipwreck story. She had said she thought it was very exciting.

'Did she mind doing the typing?' asked Virginia.

'No, not at all, bless her heart.' He looked so affectionate and indulgent when he made that re- mark that Virginia began to fear Beryl might be right. 'She reckons she owes me a favour,' Frank went on. 'This is a secret, mind, so don't tell anyone. I've been teaching her to drive—she wants to surprise her mum.'

Virginia said nothing.

'She hasn't got a father of her own,' Frank ex- plained apologetically, 'and her boy-friend only has a bike.'

'That's very kind of you,' Virginia said at last.

'No, it's not,' Frank contradicted. 'I *like* doing it. I *like* youngsters. I often stay behind to teach the apprentices. I'm a teacher manqué, if you know what I mean. Or a social worker manqué, or some- thing like that.'

'I think you like being a father figure,' Virginia teased lightly.

Immediately, Frank's face clouded. 'Yes, maybe

you're right. But it wouldn't be fair to clip Beryl's wings, would it?' He seemed on the point of saying more and then changed his mind.

But the following day, Virginia had other things on her mind than the problems of Frank and Beryl. When she came down for breakfast Beryl, still in her dressing gown, was standing in the kitchen, waiting for the kettle to boil and reading the morning paper. An item had caught her attention and she was reading it wide-eyed and open-mouthed. Suddenly she threw down the paper, clapped her hands and shouted, 'Yippee!' She rushed over and embraced Virginia.

'Oh, my dear, I'm so glad!' she said, kissing her on both cheeks. 'This is what I'd hoped for! And by the way, I'm sorry I was so horrid yesterday. I didn't mean it. You put your finger on a sore point, that was all. I felt guilty all the way up to Edinburgh and back. And I'm *so* pleased for you. I knew it would work out, in the end.'

As soon as she could interrupt, Virginia said, 'I don't know what you're talking about, Beryl.'

'You don't? Really?' Beryl let out another delighted cry. 'Then let me have the honour of being the first to tell you. A piece of good news!' She seized the morning paper, opened it excitedly at the right page and unfolded it at the appropriate spot. 'Read that, dear Ginny, *read that!*'

She held the paper so enthusiastically close to Virginia's eyes that she had to squint to read the words. 'Read it aloud, Ginny dear.'

But Virginia shook her head. It was traumatic enough reading the words to herself. Under the heading Announcements were the lines, 'The marriage arranged between Mrs Antonia Villiers and Dr Peter Willoughby will not now take place.'

'Not just *postponed*,' Beryl smiled. 'Won't take place. Final. Finished!'

'So you've had your way?' said Dr Tranter, pleasantly enough. He had just put his head round Virginia's door to say that he would be tied up with aircrew medicals till noon. There was a *Daily Telegraph* tucked into the pocket of his white coat, and he tapped it as he made his unforgivable remark.

When she said nothing, and simply sat stony-faced, Dr Tranter added in that pleasant cool unimpassioned voice he so often used to her, 'I see Peter Willoughby finally took your advice.'

'I think he's quite capable of making up his own mind.' Even to her own ears that sounded unconvincing.

'Do you? Myself, I doubt that.'

He closed the door behind him, and she heard his brisk footsteps fading down the corridor. She heard him cheerfully bidding goodbye to Night Sister Porter, as she called, 'Hubby's here!' and hurried away.

Then the phone began ringing and the tide of the day's duties swept Virginia's thoughts away from the Chief and Peter Willoughby and Mrs Villiers. At lunchtime she managed to eat a sandwich and drink the coffee Rosie made for her in the little section kitchen.

As Rosie refilled her cup she asked cheerfully, 'Did you read the paper this morning?' and when Virginia merely looked aghast she went on, 'There was a big piece in it about Clare's fiancé. He's been sighted, well on his way home. Wonderful, isn't it?'

At two o'clock Virginia was summoned out on an urgent call to a departing transatlantic aircraft. Hurrying through Reception, she met Dr Tranter and Clare on their way to do the afternoon's aircrew medicals, and without intentionally eavesdropping, she heard Dr Tranter say, 'Allow him to settle back first, Clare, then break it to him. Don't be precipitate.'

Virginia wished she could have stopped her ears up with cotton wool and averted her eyes from the proud tender look which Clare beamed on him. Though why she should mind, she didn't allow herself to think. They were totally unaware of her. They didn't even throw her a backward glance, as she fled up the Cord and over to the Departures Lounge.

The Traffic girl who had called her out had given her only the barest information. An elderly gentleman travelling to Los Angeles was, in the opinion of the aircraft Captain, quite unfit to fly. He was accompanied by an equally elderly wife, and both of them, according to the Captain, looked as if a puff of wind would blow them away. The passenger insisted on going, and the Captain was holding up the flight until medical opinion decided.

Virginia arrived at the Departures Lounge, to be met by a very harassed Traffic Officer. The old gentleman, he told her, had almost passed out climbing up the steps to board the aircraft. Everyone thought he was going to have a heart attack, and the stewardesses had been in a fair old panic. But there he was now, sitting it out, refusing to budge, and the Captain refusing to take off.

The Traffic Officer hurried Virginia through the Departure gate, and across the tarmac.

'Try to make them see sense, Sister,' he gasped, hurrying up the aircraft steps behind her.

'I'll do my best.' Virginia squeezed her way past two stewardesses looking on anxiously, to where a very old couple, dressed neatly in old-fashioned dark grey suits, sat grim-faced staring ahead of them. The aircraft was three-quarters full, but they were separated from the rest of the passengers by a row of empty seats. Leaning, with attempted casualness, across the back of the seat immediately in front of them, was the equally grim-faced Captain. He was a tall rubicund man who looked as if his normal expression might be reasonable. But today he was fiery with frustration and irritation.

He wasted no words.

'For heaven's sake, Sister, get them to see we're doing the best for them. And let the rest of us get cracking!'

At that, the little old woman replied in a high quavery voice that was nevertheless incisive, 'In that case, Captain, you should take us to where we want to go. We've bought our tickets. *We've* done our part, now you do *your's*!'

The Captain made a gesture of beating his head with his fists.

'No one said when we booked that we looked too old and shaky. Besides, we've *got* to go.'

'If I might just say something?' Virginia put in. 'And if we could have a little privacy? The first class section usually isn't so full mid-week?'

Thankfully, perhaps glad to see that the elderly

couple hadn't actually taken root, the Captain led them into the almost empty first class section. Virginia sat herself down beside them and introduced herself.

More relaxed that at least they were not now being stared at by hundreds of other fellow passengers, the elderly couple gave their names as Mr and Mrs Stanfield. They told Virginia that the object of their journey was to visit their daughter, who was seriously ill in Los Angeles, and nothing was going to stop them.

Certainly Mr Stanfield was very short of breath, but he was excited—it was the first time they had flown, and anyway, they had a letter from their GP saying he was fit to fly. Mrs Stanfield dipped her small gloved hand into her big black handbag and brought it out.

'Mr Stanfield,' Virginia asked gently, 'would you mind if I gave you a little examination? I would need to before I could say one way or the other.'

The couple put their heads together and conferred.

'Just heart, lungs . . . that sort of thing,' she added.

Reluctantly the couple signified their compliance by a simultaneous nod.

'My lungs,' Mr Stanfield admitted with wheezy dignity, 'are not as good as they were sixty years ago.' He coughed apologetically. 'My doctor says it's just *anno domini*—wearing away.'

'Emphysema,' Virginia murmured, listening carefully.

'Yes. But I've still enough breath to get to Los Angeles and back.'

Virginia looked thoughtful but said nothing.

'And,' Mr Stanfield continued, 'there's not much wrong with the old ticker, is there, considering it's been going for eighty-odd years?'

'And if we don't go now,' Mrs Stanfield clenched her little black-gloved fists, 'it'll be never.'

'Nevertheless,' Virginia said gently, 'I must ask you to accept my decision, whatever it is.' She put away her stethoscope, closed her emergency bag, and prayed for wisdom.

She was not sure that her prayer was answered, for the pros and cons of letting the Stanfields go or offloading them were so evenly balanced. Perhaps wisdom would have told her to interrupt Dr Tranter and call him out to make the difficult decision. But he had assured her that her ability in diagnosis, and quick diagnosis at that, was good, and she intended to live up to that opinion.

Besides, time, she knew, counted. The aircraft would lose its place in the take-off queue and the crowded air-lanes. The Captain was already impatient and the other passengers angrily querying why they weren't leaving.

Virginia stood up. The Captain was waiting just outside the first class section. 'Well, Sister?'

She cleared her throat, expecting trouble. 'In my opinion,' she said, 'Mr Stanfield *is* fit to travel, Captain. I feel they've bought their tickets and should be carried. I'd like you to allow them to stay in the first class section—and take an extra cylinder of oxygen. But I think he'll make it, because he's determined to make it.'

To her surprise, the Captain shrugged and spread his hands, but didn't argue. He gave her a small rueful smile. 'Well, I hope you're right, Sister. I'll take your word for it, as if it was spoken by your Chief himself. But if we've got to turn back halfway across the Atlantic because the old boy's taken ill, your head will roll. And it'll be your Chief himself who sees it rolls!'

It rolled long before that. Virginia didn't return to the section until the aircraft had taxied to the end of the runway. She caught a glimpse, as the steps were pulled, away of a little black-gloved hand enthusiastically waving from behind the window in the first class, then she returned to her office.

Every time the emergency telephone rang, she feared it would be Operations to say that an aircraft was returning with a dying passenger aboard.

The phone rang frequently, and with even greater frequency, Virginia glanced at the clock. When Rosie brought her a cup of tea, she thought, now the Stanfields will be more than halfway across the Atlantic. She was just expanding her report on the Stanfields for Night Sister when Richard Tranter came in.

He walked over and stood behind her, reading her entries in the log, over her shoulder. He leaned forward, the better to do so, and his sleeve brushed her cheek as he pointed to the Stanfield entry.

'You let them travel!' he exclaimed.

'Yes.'

'A man of eighty-three with emphysema and a wife equally old?'

'Yes.'

'Why?'

'There were extenuating circumstances.'

'There are no such things as circumstances, extenuating or otherwise. Either a passenger is fit to travel or he isn't. It's a medical opinion you have to give, not an emotional one.'

'You can't always separate them!'Virginia contradicted. 'They had strong reasons for getting to Los Angeles.'

'The Captain and the other passengers also have strong reasons for getting to Los Angeles. Did you consider what would happen if he was taken seriously ill?'

'Yes, of course I did.'

'What do you suppose would happen?'

Virginia answered steadily, 'If he were very ill, I suppose the aircraft would turn back.'

'And do you know what that involves, besides delays and disruptions to all the other passengers?'

'I don't know what it involves in detail, no.'

'Well, I'll tell you. It involves jettisoning the fuel before they can land back here. That's literally throwing away thousands of pounds. Then just the turning round of a large aircraft is expensive. They might also have to call out another crew because of Flight Time Limitations, and there's the inconvenience to the hundred or so other people on board.'

'But against that,' Virginia said stoutly, 'on the other side of the coin, I believed he could get there. I believed he was fit to fly. The Stanfields knew that if they didn't go to visit their daughter now, they never would. And they were absolutely determined.'

'So in the final instance, you allowed your heart to rule your head?'

'No! My head told me that determination is more than half the battle. If someone really wants to do something, they'll do it. Where there's a will, there's a way.'

Glancing up, she saw the expression in his eyes momentarily soften as if he understood both her dilemma and her decision. Then he seemed to remember something he had briefly allowed himself to forget. His deep voice took on a biting edge.

Unforgivably, he said, 'Ah, of course, I was forgetting your belief in that dictum.' He paused. 'Where there's a will there's a way. *Your* way.'

And without another word, he walked out and closed the door.

CHAPTER TWELVE

BERYL opened the door of Number Seven before Virginia had a chance to put her key in the door. 'You've just missed Peter,' she said. 'He's phoned three times already.'

Virginia said nothing for a moment. Perhaps because she was tired, or worried about the Stanfields, or distressed by Dr Tranter's anger, or a combination of all three, she felt thankful not to have to talk to Peter.

When Beryl continued to look at her expectantly, she asked, 'Did he leave a message?'

'Yes, he did,' Beryl beamed happily. 'First of all, he asked if we'd read this morning's *Daily Telegraph*. I told him we had. I asked him if it had been a difficult decision, and he said no, all in all, he felt it had worked out best all round.'

'He wasn't heartbroken?' Virginia took off her cape and hung it up.

'No fear! He seemed relieved. He's invited us all out to dinner this evening,' Beryl added, 'at Entwick Manor.'

'I'm afraid . . .' Virginia began, when Beryl caught her hand. 'Oh, please, Ginny, no excuses! Don't say you won't go. I've never been to Entwick Manor. I rang Frank at work and he says he'll come. Frank and I . . . well, it'll be like old times.'

Virginia had not the heart to protest any further. She allowed herself to be led upstairs to decide which dress Beryl should wear.

'I thought of this,' Beryl held against herself a silk dress of soft greens and browns. 'It isn't new, but Frank likes me in these colours. Or is this better?' She hauled out from the wardrobe a red woollen dress with a cowl neck and a black patent leather belt. 'I've got some very high-heeled patent leather shoes to wear with it.'

'No, I like the first one better,' Virginia decided, determined that Beryl should wear what Frank liked. If nothing else came out of this evening, at least it might help heal the relationship between Frank and Beryl. Beryl accepted her dictum without question.

'If I wash my hair now,' she asked, 'will you set it for me? Peter said unless he heard to the contrary, he'd pick us up at eight.'

Virginia nodded and followed her into the bathroom. 'Is Peter driving down specially?'

'To be honest,' said Beryl, pinning a towel round her shoulders, 'specially to see *you*.' She unhooked the spray nozzle and began drenching her hair.

'I'm not at all sure *I* want to see *him*,' said Virginia doubtfully.

'Oh, it's early days yet—I told him so.' Beryl rubbed in some shampoo vigorously. 'He said you'd feel like that. He knows you're a sensitive soul. But it's not your fault his engagement's come to nothing. It *couldn't* work out. The marriage would have been a total disaster. It's chalk and cheese, with Crispin sandwiched in the middle. Besides, Peter reckons she's still fond of her husband.'

Virginia said nothing for several minutes.

'Soon the whole engagement,' Beryl went on, determinedly rinsing away the shampoo suds, as if she were rinsing away the entire past, 'will be water under the bridge. Then perhaps . . .' Conscious of Virginia's silence, she left the rest unsaid, while Virginia towelled her hair and began setting it in rollers.

Peter arrived before Virginia had finished changing into an apricot dress she had bought in the Sales just before leaving London. From her bedroom window she watched his car draw up, and after a moment, Peter himself got out. She waited for that remembered catch of her heart at the sight of him, his fair hair gently ruffled, bleached in the light of the street lamp. But nothing happened. Her heartbeat remained steady. She watched him as someone watching a stranger, as he ran a comb quickly through his hair, and then bent inside the car to bring out two cellophane cartons. A few months ago, Peter arriving with what looked like orchids would have seemed to her the summit of human happiness. Now she simply thought *Beryl will be pleased*.

Beryl was enchanted. For her at least, it set the evening on the right note. Frank was already downstairs, dressed stiffly in his good grey suit, entertaining Peter to a glass of sherry. Both men raised their glasses gallantly as the girls descended, and Peter presented the orchids with exaggerated bows.

'Pin Ginny's on for her, Peter,' smiled Beryl. 'It goes beautifully with her dress. Frank'll do mine.'

As Beryl had no doubt intended, Peter also planted a long lingering kiss on Virginia's lips, and kept his arm possessively round her waist till they went out to the car.

'You two marrieds can sit in the back and hold hands,' he told Beryl and Frank.

'I expect,' Beryl said, 'you and Ginny have got a lot to say to one another.'

But Virginia could think of nothing. What mind she had seemed firmly fixed on the day's doings at the section, on Dr Tranter's manifest hostility to her, and the fate of the Stanfields. All she could think of to ask Peter was had he seen Crispin, but he replied sharply, 'No, thank heaven! I've kept out of the monster's way.' And in the uncomfortable silence, Beryl took it upon herself to keep the conversation going. She talked about her trip to Edinburgh, the pranks the children had got up to, and airline gossip.

'Talking of gossip,' she said, leaning forward, 'did you see that other item of interest in this morning's paper?'

Not waiting for anyone to answer yea or nay, she went on, 'The bit about Donald Cunningham—the round-the-world yachtsman.'

'Yes, I saw that,' her husband answered. 'He's doing well, making good time. He's a brave chap. But what's the gossip in *that*?'

'*Dear* Frank!' Beryl sighed. 'He never listens when I gossip. I'm sure I must have told you —certainly I've told Ginny. When Donald Cunningham gets home, our Clare Todd is going to break off her engagement to him and marry our Dr Tranter.'

Frank clicked his tongue in mingled disapproval and disbelief, but Peter said loudly, 'It wouldn't surprise me.' He paused. 'Though I can't think what makes her fall for Tranter. She's one of the most attractive girls I've ever seen.'

That remark caused the conversation to falter again. 'You've got *the* most attractive girl sitting beside you right now,' Beryl, still bent on her role of matchmaker, reminded Peter gaily.

'Of course I have,' he replied with what sounded like forced enthusiasm, removing his left hand from the wheel and patting Virginia's folded ones. 'She knows me too well to be jealous, don't you, darling?'

'Much too well,' Virginia answered with a dry significance that was for her ears only. For she was jealous. She, who would have sworn a few months ago that jealousy was alien to her nature, now found herself in the grip of that humiliating and detestable emotion.

Staring at the lights on the road ahead, listening to the soft sound of the car engine, and the swish of the tyres, she admitted guiltily to herself that she was jealous of Clare Todd, of her beauty, of her power to get her own way, and most of all of the place she held in Richard Tranter's affections. In mingled relief and wistfulness she realised that she was cured of any infatuation she had had for Peter, that she had been in love with someone she had invented, not a real person. That probably now she would never marry. And that she would trade any man's love to be held in high regard and respect by the Chief.

Then they arrived at Entwick Manor, and the first person they saw in the hall was Richard Tranter. He was dressed in a well cut grey suit, as if out for the evening, and he looked as perturbed at seeing her as she no doubt did at seeing him. Virginia felt herself give a visible start, partly because he had been so much in her thoughts, but mostly because that catch of the heart, so absent from when she had seen Peter again, now threatened her like some mysterious delayed shock.

Having just told herself that she was cured of love and resolved to settle for regard and respect, she now found herself the victim of a far more lethal strain of the disease.

She half hoped Richard would turn away as they came in, but there was no way in which they could politely avoid each other. Virginia was acutely and uncomfortably aware of his eyes on her face, of his unhurried gaze, taking in their formal clothes, the orchids, the celebratory air that surrounded them all. Momentarily, his expression darkened.

Peter seemed blissfully unaware of any hostility in the atmosphere or to be abashed by Dr Tranter's curt nod. He walked over and greeted him with cheerful deference. 'Hello, sir, nice to see you again. Are you dining here as well?'

'No.' Richard Tranter gazed down at Peter from his superior height and shook his head. 'I'm just here on an errand—a brief errand.'

He half turned as if subconsciously indicating that this was all he intended saying and that somehow the little party was intruding on his privacy.

Then from the direction of the Manager's office, Virginia saw Clare Todd walking smilingly towards them. She was followed by the rotund figure of the

Manager, walking importantly and carrying a large folder under his arm.

'I think, sir,' said the Manager, addressing himself to Dr Tranter, 'that I have everything here you were wanting. I've pencilled in the likely date Miss Todd has given me. Please take this folder with you. You'll find quotations for the champagne and the food at the reception. Pore over it at your leisure, sir. Then if you let me know how large the reception is going to be . . .'

Feeling themselves unwanted, they all, even Peter, moved away. 'Well', said Beryl, as they settled themselves in at the dinner table, 'the gossip was right all along, wasn't it? *Now* do you believe me, Frank? We've just had it straight from the horse's mouth. A wedding reception is being arranged!'

The following morning, half an hour after Virginia arrived, Richard Tranter came into her office and took it into his head to apologise on two counts. After expressing the hope, in a clipped manner, that she had enjoyed her celebration dinner, *for whatever it was they were celebrating*—He paused there for a moment as if inviting her to explain the celebration, and when she remained silent, went on to apologise for any brusqueness of manner on his part. 'As it happens,' he said, 'Clare and I were pressed for time and we had several arrangements to make.'

Virginia inclined her head to show she understood, and in an equally clipped manner assured him that she had not noticed any brusqueness.

'No doubt you were not in a mood to notice.'

'Possibly not.'

On the second count, Dr Tranter was more forthcoming. 'The Stanfields,' he began, thrusting his hands into the pockets of his white coat and staring down at her with a baffling expression.

She swivelled her chair round to stare at him wide-eyed. 'What about them?' she breathed nervously.

He gave her a strange almost tender little smile, then announced, 'They arrived safely.'

'Oh, that's wonderful!' She jumped to her feet. For a perilous moment she felt as if she could fling her arms round him.

'I thought you'd be pleased.' His eyes crinkled up at her pleasure.

'I'm delighted. When did you hear?'

'I asked Ops Los Angeles to telex me. The telex has just come in.'

'Thank you,' she murmured, her voice husky with relief. 'It was kind of you to go to the trouble to find out.'

'Oh, don't thank me,' he said with pretended gruffness. 'I simply wanted to know the section hadn't made an almighty blunder.'

But Virginia was not totally deceived. She saw the expression in his eyes, and the deepening of the little lines round his mouth. 'You're teasing me?'

'Not entirely.'

'You're as pleased as I am.'

He didn't answer.

'And not just because the section didn't blunder.'

He still said nothing.

After a moment she asked hopefully, 'Did Ops say how the daughter is?'

Dr Tranter nodded. 'Her condition is so far unchanged. She's stabilised.' He smiled. 'No doubt the Stanfields' advent will cause a significant improvement.'

'I do hope so!' Virginia clasped her hands together.

'If what I hear about their determination is true, they'll *will* her better,' Richard Tranter said lightly, 'by sheer determination.'

Virginia laughed, 'I think you're right.'

He smiled at her pleasure and relief. She knew he shared these feelings with her. Just for a moment a beguiling sense of total empathy seemed to enfold them.

'And with hindsight, your decision was the right one.' He put his hand on her shoulder. 'I apologise for doubting it.'

A long time ago Virginia's grandmother had said, it takes a strong man to be able to apologise to a subordinate, and an even stronger one when that subordinate is a woman.

Virginia found herself totally unable to say anything. She had to beam all her concentration on trying not to cover Richard's hand with hers. Even if she could have spoken she would have been afraid to break the moment's spell. Then the telephone rang and the moment shattered. She was recalled to life and their roles in it again.

He took his hand from her shoulder to pick up the telephone.

She heard, from the other end, the loud voice of the Operations Officer.

Dr Tranter listened intently. A slight frown of concentration drew his dark brows together.

As if feeling her eyes on his face, he looked up suddenly. 'We're both going to be needed on this one,' he said, pressing the button on the desk that would summon the airline ambulance.

'Resuscitation kit?' she asked him.

'Obstetric kit,' and then into the telephone, 'Are they sure? Who's examined her? Has the stewardess any nursing experience? How far out is the aircraft?' He listened for a few more seconds and said, 'Right. I take it Control will direct us,' and put down the receiver.

He turned to Virginia, 'A young woman on an incoming Far East flight. She's begun premature labour. The Captain thought they could land in time, but he was wrong.'

Dr Tranter walked through into the treatments room and began selecting instruments from the steriliser. Over his shoulder he threw, 'The young woman's in a state of collapse and the Captain reckons the baby is already dead.'

He continued the conversation as they climbed into the ambulance. 'The baby was in the breech position. There's no doctor among the passengers. The stewardesses have done a first aid course, but none of them has had nursing experience.' He stared angrily out at the green waste grass between the runways as the ambulance sped them round the perimeter. 'I often wonder why people in the airline business put so much weight on glamour.'

In happier, less fraught circumstances, Virginia might have thought wryly that Dr Tranter himself seemed to put a good deal of weight on glamour.

Who could be more glamorous than the dazzling Clare Todd? But she knew that he was simply letting off his frustration and anger at a new life lost for want of skilled help.

'How many months pregnant was she?' Virginia asked.

'Seven or eight months—the Captain wasn't sure. He says the husband was stationed out there, building bridges. They wanted the baby born at home in England.'

'And how long before the aircraft lands?'

Dr Tranter looked at his watch. 'About another three minutes. Control has cleared the air lanes and they've been given top priority. They'll be the next one down.' He screwed up his eyes against the bright light of the sun, and Virginia studied his calm determined profile as he scanned the rounded white build-ups of cumulus cloud for the first sight of an aircraft.

She held her breath. And with her, the whole airport seemed to hold its breath too. There came a lull in the normal continuous roar of aircraft landing and taking off. In the quiet, she could hear only the distant hum of motor traffic and the nearer twittering of birds in the grass between the runways. It seemed truly amazing and heartwarming and comforting that this whole vast modern jet-age complex should pause to tilt the balance between life and death for one small scrap of life up there.

In that breath-held pause the sudden roar of an approaching aircraft sounded unnaturally and terrifyingly loud.

'There she is!' Dr Tranter put his hand on her arm and pointed to a silver fish shape emerging from beneath a distant white cavern of cloud. 'Coming straight in, by the look of her.' He turned to the ambulance driver. 'You'd better get our directions from Control, Ted.'

The ambulance driver was already turning the R/T switch near the dashboard. A voice suddenly burst out at them, 'Ambulance to proceed to Number Seven Apron now. Medical team to approach landed aircraft only when signalled to.'

'Roger,' said the driver, and stood on the accelerator.

From the side window, they saw the aircraft coming in over the approach lights. Then it was whistling above their heads as they passed Bays One and Two. Glancing up at its shiny silver underbelly, Virginia wondered what awaited them there.

'Landed safely,' said Dr Tranter, peering down the gap between two hangars. 'And a smooth landing, thank heaven!'

Through the half-open window of the ambulance, they felt the whoosh of warm air, as the aircraft's engines went into reverse thrust—then the aircraft swung away out of their sight.

They caught a glimpse of her again as they raced past Bay Number Six, still taxiing. Then she was just ahead of them into Bay Seven, swinging round slowly to tuck her tail in.

'We'll have to stop now, Ted, until she cuts engines, and we get the signal.'

In the quietness, Dr Tranter turned to Virginia. 'It may not be possible to move the patient.' He touched her hand. 'We'll probably have to do what we can where we can.'

'Aircraft's cut engines, doc,' said the driver.

'Ah, and there it is.' Dr Tranter pointed. 'We've got the green light. OK, Ted, let's go!'

As the driver pressed on the accelerator and the ambulance closed the distance between them and the aircraft, Dr Tranter still held Virginia's hand. She had never before known what calm and resolution such a small gesture could bring.

There was a moment's pause while the aircraft steps were wheeled into place. A small bald-headed man in the uniform of the Port Health Authority followed them up, as the aircraft doors were thrown open.

A stewardess, very pale under her make-up, waved them into the curtained off area usually reserved as a stewardesses' rest room. 'Thank heavens you're here!' she whispered.

They had made the patient as comfortable as they could, covered her with blankets and given her a knotted towel to bear down on. She was writhing in pain, biting the pillow, her face dripping with sweat.

Their appearance immediately calmed her, as if Dr Tranter's white coat and Virginia's uniform had brought all the reassurance of a modern hospital. Everyone was eager to help. A steward brought up their kit, while a stewardess rushed off to get towels.

'Now, my dear—' Gently Dr Tranter bent over the young woman to make his examination. Over his shoulder, Virginia could see that the baby's buttocks already seemed to have appeared and that they were an unhealthy blue. Her heart sank. As she unpacked the obstetrics kit, she looked around at the tiny confines in which they were to work—and work so fast.

Time seemed simultaneously to telescope and expand. She put a cold compress on the young woman's forehead and opened her bag. She became an automaton. Never had she thought two people could work so swiftly and in such silent harmony. Never had she felt such complete empathy with anyone. It was as if she had never known Dr Tranter till this moment. Now she had become the companion of his thoughts, privy to his decisions, and now her hands were moved not so much by her mind as his.

About to hand him the forceps, she paused and watched instead as his long fingers fastened over the little buttocks—thrusting, twisting, pulling with delicate and consummate skill.

'Push,' she whispered to the young woman. 'We're almost there.' She fastened the mask over her face. 'Just breathe naturally,' she said soothingly. 'In a moment . . .'

But what would happen in a moment, she didn't know. Too late, delivered of a stillborn child, she thought sadly, seeing Dr Tranter withdraw the tiny purple body and sever and clamp the cord.

Time stood still. Then what seemed a little miracle happened. There came a thin cry that echoed electrifyingly down the cave of the aircraft. The pale-faced stewardess was handing Dr Tranter towels and blankets, tears streaking her make-up. For a moment, as she attended to the patient, Virginia wondered if she had imagined the baby's cry, for everyone seemed to be crying. Even the Captain, hovering outside the curtained-off area, was blowing his nose loudly.

'Tell her she has a daughter,' Dr Tranter said with the brusqueness that she had learned masked his deepest emotions. 'And let's hope she'll be more sensible than her mother!'

Drowsily, contentedly, the young woman smiled.

'We'll pack them straight off in the ambulance. It can drop us at the section on the way.' Dr Tranter bent down over the young mother as she beckoned that she had something to whisper in his ear. He listened intently, a strange gentle smile playing round his lips.

'Virginia,' he said aloud.

Virginia turned to look at him in surprise—not just that he spoke her name but that he spoke it with such tenderness.

He explained, 'The patient wants to know your Christian name. She intends to call the baby after you.' He put the blanket-wrapped baby in Virginia's arms, and gave her a smile of extra-ordinary sweetness. Then he bent down and picked up the patient and carried her to the waiting ambulance. When the ambulance had dropped them off, Dr Tranter and Virginia stood side by side for a moment outside the section, watching the flashing blue light of the ambulance disappearing rapidly in the direction of the County Hospital.

They seemed isolated in a mysterious world of their own, too profound for mere words, too exciting, too deeply personal for anyone else to enter, and more intimate than love itself. Virginia was afraid to speak. In silence, they returned to her office, and Dr Tranter closed the door behind them.

'Virginia . . . ?' he began in a tone of voice she had never heard him use before. Then he stopped.

After the most perfunctory of knocks, Clare Todd put her head round the door. 'Oh, you're back—good! Mind if I interrupt the tête-à-tête for a moment? Everything go all right?' And without waiting for an answer to either question, in she came.

She was smiling happily. She carried the file from the Entwick Manor Hotel under her arm.

CHAPTER THIRTEEN

THE following Saturday evening, Frank and Beryl dined again at Entwick Manor. This time the dinner was a real and very personal celebration—their seventh wedding anniversary.

'I can't get over the fact that Frank booked the table without even asking me!' Beryl said to Virginia on the Sunday morning afterwards.

It was Virginia's day off, and they were enjoying a leisurely cup of coffee, while Frank worked in the garden mowing the lawn and taking some geranium cuttings.

'He's just not that sort of person. As for remembering it was our wedding anniversary . . . ! Well, you could have knocked me down with a feather. Funny that I should have been grumbling to you the other week that he's never remembered an anniversary in all our married life.'

'Frank's a good deal more thoughtful than you give him credit for,' Virginia suggested, as Beryl's eye regarded her with sudden suspicion.

'Or someone else put him up to it.'

'Who would possibly do that?'

'You wouldn't have reminded him, would you?'

'Me? Good heavens,' Virginia exclaimed in her best Sister Casualty tone, 'I have many more important things to remind people of . . .' But she was spared the necessity of even a white lie, for Beryl put down her cup and said, 'Oh, yes, that reminds *me*. Guess who we saw at Entwick Manor?'

'Dr Tranter?'

'No. Though I'm sure he was somewhere around. We saw Clare, in consultation with the Manager again. He looked pretty harassed. This time they were talking floral arrangements, and she actually came over and spoke to us.'

'Maybe you'll get invited to the wedding.'

'I doubt that—we're not grand enough for her. She didn't come over to improve our acquaintance. She came over to ensure we kept mum.'

'What about?'

'The reception, of course. To use her own words: We wouldn't want my fiancé to find out before I tell him.'

'Oh,' said Virginia flatly.

'Yes—my very word. I was speechless. Then she gave me a little homily about airline gossip, and about how it usually manages to get hold of the wrong end of the stick . . . though I think she's wrong there . . . and how everything depended on this being a secret till the right moment.'

'What did you say?'

'Well, privately I thought it very hard-nosed of her. But I said she could rely on us. I don't want the poor fellow to hear any rumours before he's strong enough to take what's coming to him.'

'That satisfied her, I hope?'

'Not quite. She then murmured enquiringly about *you*. I said you're discretion itself, but Frank piped up with a real paean of praise . . . About how discreet and kind and thoughtful you are . . . you're quite sure you didn't remind him about our wedding anniversary . . . ? Never mind . . . on he went, praising you to the sky. And ever such a funny look came into Clare's face. She said quite sharply to Frank, You'd better not let the Chief hear you say all that.'

Virginia drank another cup of coffee in total silence before asking, 'Why? Why do you think she said that?'

Beryl shrugged. 'I don't know. She's very spoiled, very demanding. She doesn't like anyone to be praised but her.'

'But why should the Chief *not* want me to be praised either?'

Beryl patted her knee. 'Don't take it to heart. Maybe you and he were a bit at cross-purposes. I know you do cross swords from time to time. Maybe it was something she made up, said on the spur of the moment. Frank and I talked about it after she'd gone and we couldn't really make head nor tail of it. Though I must say Frank did have a theory.'

'Which was?'

'Oh, he wouldn't tell me. He said it was something to do with a man's feelings and something women would never understand.'

'We have to be very understanding of Clare Todd at the moment,' Richard Tranter said the following week, as Virginia and he left the medical section together. 'She's under great strain, and this outburst was a symptom of it.'

The outburst in question had just taken place. Clare Todd had burst into tears because a phone call she had been about to take, apparently from Ireland, had suddenly gone off the line. She had expressed the determination to go to Rosie's PBX and stay with her there to make sure it didn't happen again. She had refused Dr Tranter's offer to accompany her. And though he now addressed his remarks to Virginia, it seemed to be himself he was reminding. 'Each time the phone rings she thinks it's news of Donald.'

'I realise that,' Virginia said stiffly.

'She's tremendously keyed up for his arrival.'

'And for what follows it,' Virginia heard herself exclaim—and could have bitten her tongue.

Dr Tranter shot her a quizzical sideways glance. 'Put baldly like that, yes, I suppose so.' But his expression was impenitent as if he didn't feel the slightest tinge of guilt for the news that was to be broken to the yachtsman on his return. 'It's been a long-drawn-out strain for her all this last year.'

'I'm sure you've done your best to support her!' The words were wrung out of her. They had reached the car park, and Virginia began to walk briskly ahead of him, willing him to mount his bicycle and go away. But instead, he put his hand on her arm to restrain her.

'Why did you say that?' he demanded.

'Because it's true.' She fumbled in her handbag for her car keys.

'But why with such feeling, Virginia?' Reaching the car, he bent down to open the door for her.

Securely inside, she said through he open window, 'I was not aware that I said it with any feeling. In fact I have no feeling whatever in the matter.' And when he looked surprised, 'What feeling did you suppose I had?'

He raised his brows quizzically. 'It seemed to me—' he paused and finished softly, 'the feeling was jealousy.'

'Jealousy! *Jealousy!*' Her eyes sparkled with indignation. 'Why on earth should I be jealous of Clare?'

'That's what *I* wondered.'

Ignoring that, Virginia thrust the key in the ignition and turned it with trembling fingers.

The car, which these days seemed to have a will of its own, refused to allow her to make a dignified withdrawal. When she pulled out the choke and tried again it gave a groan of protest, a tired cough, then fell into an ominous silence.

'Let me help,' Dr Tranter opened the driver's door. 'Move over. Give me the keys.' He plucked them from her unprotesting fingers, but he didn't immediately try the ignition. 'Let's give it a rest for a moment, shall we? You've probably flooded the carburettor.' He gave her a little sideways, almost self-deprecating smile. 'That's my diagnosis.' His smile became reminiscent. 'As you rightly said the first time we met, you get to know a lot about engines working on an airport.'

'Ah, then I thought you were a mechanic.' She smiled in spite of her indignation. After a while she added, 'I'm surprised you remembered.'

He looked at her intently. '*Are* you?'

'Yes.'

'I've remembered . . .' he spoke softly, 'so much.'

For a moment neither of them spoke. Virginia held her breath, fearful that he would go on, and equally fearful that he would not.

He went on softly, 'Working together one gets to know people very well.'

It was an obvious statement and yet spoken as if it were of profound importance. Virginia twisted her hands in her lap and nodded. She was not sure where all this was leading. All she knew was that an illusory hope flared, and as quickly died. She reminded herself bleakly that this was probably leading to an explanation of how he and Clare Todd had fallen in love and to bring him back to his original plea that everyone had to be patient with Clare.

Painfully, she heard him continue in that same quiet reminiscent tone, 'Much better than, say, sharing a social life together.'

'Yes, of course,' Virginia agreed, for on this point there could be no argument. Richard glanced sideways at her expectantly. She elaborated, 'Being members of a team . . . we get to know each other's strengths and weaknesses . . .' she broke off, her voice trailing away. She was overwhelmed with a longing for him to touch her hand, to take her in his arms, to tell her all this was not leading up to why he had fallen in love with Clare.

But it was—that fact was inescapable. And before she showed her own terrible weakness, she must escape with her dignity and self-control intact. Pointedly she looked at her wrist watch. Immediately, he put the key in the ignition and turned it. The capricious car responded as sweetly as if it had been transformed into a Rolls-Royce.

'I seem to have a way with the car,' Dr Tranter said lightly, 'but not with its owner.'

Virginia turned her gaze to his half-smiling profile. 'I don't know what you mean?' she whispered.

Her eyes were wide and profoundly puzzled.

He looked down into their clear grey depths and sighed. 'I haven't made myself very clear, have I?' He slid an arm round her shoulder, and with his free hand tilted up her chin.

Then he covered her mouth with his. It was a warm, passionate, meaningful kiss, and for a few seconds she surrendered to its tenderness and passion. And because it was a kiss which a moment before she had longed for she allowed herself the dangerous illusion that he meant it.

Then she remembered that he was about to marry Clare Todd, and the illusion burst like a pretty bubble. She pushed against him with all her strength, turning her head sideways to escape his lips.

He looked surprised, angry, and then coldly withdrawn. 'I'm sorry,' he said stiffly. 'Under the circumstances, I shouldn't have . . .' he didn't finish the sentence. Then, preparing to get out of the car, he asked, to her astonishment in an almost expressionless tone, 'Have you no regard for me?'

'None!' she answered hotly, amazed and shocked and disappointed at his disloyalty. 'I respect you as a doctor. But I hate you as a man!'

It had been like talking in code, Virginia thought, lying in bed that night. For black read white, for no regard, read every regard, for hate read love. The only truth she had clearly uttered was the sentence, I respect you as a doctor. She certainly did that. But she didn't respect him as a man.

How could she? Not satisfied with making

Donald Cunningham's fiancée fall in love with him while the poor man was battling for his life, he was also expecting Virginia to fall at his feet and into his arms for managing to start her car. He was no better than Peter Willoughby. In fact, he was considerably worse. Certainly he was worse for *her*. For she knew she had only imagined herself in love with Peter, but now she knew with dreadful certainty that what she felt for Dr Richard Tranter was the real and fatal thing.

Much as she loved her job at the airport, much as she felt she belonged, she knew she would have to leave it. She could not go on working with him in such close proximity. She began looking at advertisements. She considered doing agency work, and she became altogether more formal with Dr Tranter.

The message appeared to have got through to him. And though like the code of black equals white it was the wrong message, he seemed to accept the fact that she disliked him. Whenever he saw her, he treated her with scrupulous politeness, but his eyes were grave and shadowed and he hardly ever smiled.

With the contrariness of life her work, now that she had decided she must leave it, seemed to become especially precious and rewarding. People asked for her by name. Her waiting room was nearly always full. There seemed no end to the interesting people she discovered hidden away in the airfield, nor the challenge of the different cases that called for her help.

Ten days after Richard Tranter had tried to kiss her, a great strapping man came into her office with a bloodstained face, announcing that he'd just had a fight.

'On the airport?'

''fraid so.'

'Who with?' Virginia asked disapprovingly.

'My best friend.'

'Shame on you!' Virginia beckoned him to come through to the treatments room.

'It was his fault, Sister,' the man assured her. 'He began it.'

'Was he hurt?'

'Not on your life, Sister! Didn't lose a feather.' He winced as Virginia examined deep jagged tears on his face.

'What did he hit you with?' she asked.

'Beak and claws.' He smiled at Virginia's astonished expression, found it too painful and explained, 'My friend is called King Harry. He's my pet hawk and I'm Birdie Higgs, the bird scarer. My job's to keep the runways clear of gulls and lapwings and rooks and starlings. Usually I use mechanical bangers—but birds are cunning little devils, they get to know when the banger's going to go off. So I brought in Harry.'

'What happened then?' Virginia cleaned the wounds carefully.

'All the excitement went to Harry's head and he got tangled in the netting at Dispersal. When I freed him he was so scared he went for me.'

Birdie Higgs studied Virginia's face. 'Made a bit of a mess of my beauty, hasn't he?'

She nodded. 'I don't like that gash just below your eye.' She drew a deep breath. 'I think it needs suturing.' The next words she found very hard to say. 'And I think I'd like Dr Tranter to see it.'

Birdie Higgs groaned, 'He'll bawl me out.'

'I'm sure he won't.'

'Then you don't know the Chief. He's been on at me before about King Harry, told me not to bring him on to the field. He doesn't like people who don't do what he tells them to.'

'But he likes people to be professional,' Virginia said. 'I promise you it's the only thing he really likes them to be. And you were only following your profession.' She walked across the treatments room, knocked on Dr Tranter's door and when he bade her come in, asked him politely, with her eyes lowered to the floor, if he could spare the time to come and examine a patient.

He answered equally politely, 'Of course, Sister,' jumped to his feet and followed her. When he saw Birdie Higgs, he bellowed, 'Don't tell me you've had that brute of a hawk on the airfield again?'

'Sorry, Doc. Truly I am. I won't again, I promise you. I'll find some other way.'

'Well, let's take a look at you.' The Chief's voice softened to his quiet professional tone. Carefully, he examined Mr Higgs. 'Mmm,' he said after several seconds, 'he's really had his own back, hasn't he? And a hawk's beak and claws aren't the cleanest instruments in the world. Sister's going to have to turn you into a pincushion. And if she doesn't mind, I'd like to stitch that eye.'

Virginia watched the delicacy of his fingers in silent and profound admiration. Just for a few moments she could allow professional and personal feelings to come together.

When Richard had finished, Birdie Higgs thanked him profusely and asked, 'Made me as good as new again, have you, doc?'

'Let's say,' Dr Tranter replied gruffly, 'that I've done a professional job.'

But it was to Virginia that he addressed that remark, and the resentment in his voice was more wounding than any claws.

CHAPTER FOURTEEN

No doubt, Virginia told herself, the strain of waiting was telling on Dr Tranter. Two weeks later,
a message came through on the eight o'clock
radio news that a ham radio enthusiast had picked
up a message putting the yachtsman, Donald
Cunningham, south-west of the Irish coast with a
following wind, and then Dr Tranter was full of
smiles.

By noon, an RAF Nimrod of Coastal Command
had sighted him, and when Sister Mortimer came
on duty, she had seen on the television that a whole
host of little ships were going out to escort him in.
Richard Tranter presented each member of the
staff with a bottle of champagne to drink when the
yachtsman arrived in Salmouth. Unfortunately,
Virginia would have to hold the fort for that occasion, as he was driving Clare down to Salmouth
to meet Donald. 'But no doubt you'll be able to
watch his arrival on breakfast TV before you come
to work.'

Though watching was going to be acutely painful
to her, Virginia rose half an hour earlier than usual,
and switched on the set in the sitting room. Still in
their dressing gowns, Frank and Beryl followed her
down.

It was certainly a moving sight. All the large ships
standing in the roads outside Salmouth were
dressed overall and sounding their sirens. Above

the ships flew the white bulk of the RAF Nimrod, dipping low over the waves. Then beneath all this greatness, the host of excited little ships, escorting Donald Cunningham, churning up the water, and there in the centre the tiny sail that was him.

'He must be a very proud man,' Frank said.

'But he's going to be such a sad one,' Virginia sighed.

'Yes,' murmured Beryl, and wiped her eyes.

Just at that moment, the TV camera panned to the civic reception awaiting the yachtsman. There was the Mayor, wearing his chain of office, the Mayoress, the aldermen in their civic rig. Beside them stood Clare Todd, lovelier than ever, her hair glittering in the morning sunlight, dressed in a smart cream silk suit, a rather rigid smile fixed on her lips, as she held Richard Tranter tightly by the hand.

'I don't think I can bear this,' Virginia said, but not aloud. Aloud, she suggested, 'Shall I make us a cup of tea?' and escaped into the kitchen.

While she made the tea, she could hear the announcer's cheerful voice as he described the yacht coming round to tie up. A naval band was playing *See the Conquering Hero Comes*, then *Heart of Oak* and the National Anthem. The schoolchildren were singing at the top of their voices.

The commentator was clearly excited.

'Now first to greet him, of course, is his fiancée . . . ah, here she runs forward to meet him . . . a sight worth going all the way round the world to see!'

'You mustn't miss this,' Beryl called. 'Come on,

Ginny! The tea can wait. Golly, either she's a good actress or . . .'

Reluctantly, Virginia came back into the sitting room and stood behind the sofa. She was in time to see Clare throw herself into the yachtsman's arms and hold him as if she was never going to let him go again. It was quite remarkably touching. The Mayor and the aldermen watched with fond smiles, while the Lady Mayoress dabbed her eyes. Richard Tranter, standing at a distance looked rather withdrawn, his face momentarily caught by the camera, curiously unhappy.

'Now Donald Cunningham is being congratulated by the Mayor and the Lord Lieutenant. A few words with the Lady Mayoress. Oh, and a kiss! Now he's turning to shake an old friend by the hand. His oldest friend, he tells me.' The camera panned to show the yachtsman clasping Richard Tranter by the hand, then slipping an arm round his shoulders, holding Clare close to him with the other, as if they were the two dearest people in the world to him.

Like that, in apparent harmony, the camera left them so that the commentator could interview some of the schoolchildren. They were jumping up and down with excitement. All of them said they wanted to be sailors when they grew up.

Suddenly, in a rather desperate voice, Virginia asked Beryl, 'What were you going to say when you said just now, "Either she's a good actress or . . . ?" You didn't finish the sentence.'

'Didn't I? Well, I can't remember now.'

'Try to.'

'Is it important? Oh, yes, I do know what I was

going to say. Either she's a good actress or she really does love him.'

'Donald Cunningham?'

'Yes.'

'Then what about Dr Tranter?'

'Oh, dear, there's him. It *is* a puzzle! I still think she'll marry him—the Chief.' Beryl stood up and looked at the clock. 'Time I did something about breakfast.' She became aware that Virginia was still staring at her expectantly. 'As I said in the first place, she's probably a very good actress. She could hardly tell him on the quayside. Dr Tranter was obviously dreading the moment. Did you see his face? I've never seen him look so unhappy. He must have felt a heel.'

'You don't think the grapevine could have got it all wrong, do you?' queried Virginia. 'And that Dr Tranter was just looking after her . . . just being a good friend?'

'Certainly not! Don't forget they were booking their wedding reception at Entwick Manor.' Beryl suddenly gulped. 'And talking of Entwick Manor, dear Ginny,' she clutched her stomach, 'do you have any idea what you've done?'

She hurried off to the cloakroom, and Virginia heard the sound of her being sick.

That evening, at Number Seven, they opened Richard Tranter's bottle of champagne to celebrate two things, Donald Cunningham's return and Beryl's pregnancy. Though it was very early days, she felt so sure inside herself. And Frank was at that moment upstairs repainting the spare bedroom.

'Things aren't always as they seem, are they?' Beryl confided to Virginia, as they sat up looking at the late night news. 'I really did think Frank was in love with this typist—and all he saw her as was a young kid who needed a bit of help, a daughter he'd never had. Of course Crispin helped to open my eyes . . .' she smiled musingly and wistfully. 'Oh, dear,' she sighed, 'if *only* Crispin could be happy, too!'

She was silent for a moment, brooding on Crispin's fate. Then she went on slowly, 'I wrote to his mother the other week, and asked her to let me know if Crispin's going to Cairo for half-term. I said I'd try to do that trip, and the return one.'

'Didn't she reply?'

Beryl spread her hands. 'I had a reply of sorts—a scrawl on a postcard.'

'Saying?'

'Saying thank you, but that won't be necessary.'

'So she's not going to let him go to Cairo?'

'It seems not.'

'Poor Crispin!' sighed Virginia.

'Poor Crispin indeed! And I have a lot to thank him for. A lot to thank you for too, of course.' Beryl patted Virginia's hand. 'For though I knew what I should do, I wouldn't admit it, not even to myself. I kept telling myself that the most important thing was for us both to work and get the house looking really super. Then, I suppose, after a while I got really hooked on my work, and Frank took a back seat.'

'Frank'll make a wonderful father,' Virginia smiled.

'Won't he just!'

'And you won't be all that bad a mother,' Virginia added.

'Thank you, my dear. And not for just that fulsome compliment, for putting it into words. For letting me see I was making mountains out of molehills, and getting all suspicious about Frank. For making me look at what I have to give him. And in the end, for telling me bluntly it was time we had children of our own. Which of course it was.'

'Sometimes,' Virginia smiled slowly, 'an on-looker sees most of the game.'

'True,' Beryl patted her hand. 'Like I'm quite sure you and Peter should . . .' But before she could say any more, Virginia pleaded that she must get some sleep and make an early start, for some-thing told her she had a trying day ahead.

She had, at that time, no idea just how trying. She had hardly set foot over the threshold than Rosie came out from her office, smiling broadly. 'I bet you haven't seen what's on the noticeboard, Sister?'

Virginia shook her head.

'Can you guess?'

'A new security routine? Or a new injection everybody's to have? Or someone's been parking where they shouldn't?'

'No, nothing like that, Sister. This is something nice, something exciting, something social.' Rosie beckoned Virginia over to the big noticeboard in the reception hall, in the centre of which a place had been cleared of notices about malaria and dysentery and the laws against carrying dangerous substances by air, to make room for a large gilt-edged card.

Virginia managed to read, '*Your company is requested . . .*' She caught a glimpse of the names Clare Todd and Richard Tranter and her eyes misted over. Her head swam.

'The whole section's invited. Isn't that lovely of them? It's so typical of the Chief, isn't it?' Rosie enthused. 'I shall get a new dress—I saw a lovely pink one in Grantly. I bet there'll be television cameras there, and all sorts of important people.'

'Not television cameras, surely, at a wedding!' Virginia protested.

'Oh, Sister, you haven't read it properly! It isn't a *wedding*—not yet! Do look, Sister. It's the reception to welcome that sailor home—Donald Cunningham. It's given by his fiancée and Dr Tranter. The Chief's his best friend. I saw that on the telly.'

Virginia said no more. She reached the sanctuary of her office. Sister Porter called out, 'Good morning.' She was through in the treatments room locking up the drugs cupboard.

'We had a quiet night,' she said cheerfully, coming in to drop the keys on the desk. 'The Chief'll be in later, but Clare's having the day off.' She began to put on her cape. 'Wonderful about Donald.'

'Wonderful!' Virginia echoed, pinning her cap in place as in a dream.

As in a dream she stood over Sister Porter to go through the medical log.

'No questions you want to ask me, are there?' asked Sister Porter, head on one side as she listened to a distinctive engine sound outside. 'Hubby's here.'

'No,' Virginia waved her goodbye, 'no questions.'

At least there were none which she could ask of Sister Porter. The only questions she could ask were of herself. After Sister Porter had gone, she sat for several minutes with her hands clasped in front of her, her grey eyes troubled, while those questions gabbled in her mind.

If Dr Tranter and Clare were not in love, who did he love? What had he meant when he spoke to her in the car? What had he been trying to tell her? What would he have gone on to say if she had given him any encouragement?

There her mind came to a full stop. She could not allow herself to speculate on what he might have said. She had not given him the slightest encouragement—quite the reverse. She had told him in no uncertain terms that she hated him, so in all probability he had assumed that she was still emotionally attached to Peter.

And though, at the earliest opportunity, she intended to apologise to him, she doubted if the proud arrogant Chief would ever open up his heart to her again.

But even the apology she seemed not destined to make. As if to make up for Sister Porter's quiet night, the telephone rang repeatedly with emergency calls, the waiting room filled. Virginia saw nothing of Dr Tranter till just after noon when he came into her office, and in the cold distant voice he used towards her these days, announced brusquely that he would do the outside emergencies.

'Dr Tranter?' she called, as he turned on his heel to go.

'Yes, Sister?' He spun round.

Faced with the uncompromising intensity of his eyes, the set of his mouth, Virginia could think of nothing to say. Her prepared speech vanished and she lowered her gaze to her clasped hands. The only words she found herself capable of forming were, 'I'm sorry—very sorry.'

To give him his due, Richard didn't try to make it difficult for her. He didn't try to pretend, as a lesser man might have done, that he didn't know what on earth she was talking about. Yet because he had got it all wrong, he did, without meaning to, make it difficult.

He simply answered quietly, 'Please don't apologise, Sister. It's not in any way your fault. You can't help your feelings, any more than I can help mine.'

And with that, he walked out and closed the door behind him.

It seemed that for ever the door would remain closed between them. And then just before four o'clock, Virginia rang her bell, and instead of an airport worker, a diminutive figure came in. To her astonishment and joy it was Crispin.

He was not alone. Nor indeed, he told her importantly, was he the patient. He held by the hand, and drew in protectively behind him, his mother.

'Mother,' he said to Virginia, 'needs another TAB jab. She forgets these things. And we're flying to Cairo tonight.'

'*Both* of you?' Virginia got up from behind her desk and led them through to the treatments room. She looked from one to the other.

'*Both* of us,' Mrs Villiers smiled. 'Isn't that nice? We're going to stay out there and see how we get along. I'm sure it will work this time. My husband's meeting us. And I can design my dresses just as well in Cairo as London.'

'I'm not,' Crispin announced happily, 'an—' he paused to get his tongue round the next difficult word '*unaccompanied* child any more.'

He watched benignly, as Virginia filled the hypodermic syringe, then he smiled in a protective manly way at his mother. 'Hold your arm still, Mother. Ginny won't hurt you.'

'I'm sure she won't,' Mrs Villiers murmured. 'Ginny is very kind.' She turned to Virginia apologetically. 'Though I wouldn't blame you if you did. I shouldn't have said what I did—but I was overwrought. I realise now you were only trying to help with Crispin.'

She closed her eyes theatrically for a moment as the needle went in.

Neither she nor Virginia noticed that the door from the other side of the treatments room had opened and that Dr Tranter had come quietly in. He stood silently where he was, arms folded across his chest, apparently waiting for the treatment to finish.

'And I realise,' Mrs Villiers went on, 'that you certainly didn't want Peter back. Not at all. That you weren't in love with him.'

'No,' Virginia said quietly. 'That's all over, a long time ago.'

Mrs Villiers nodded several times as if this went for her too. 'One day, no doubt, he'll meet the right girl.' Then she noticed Dr Tranter. 'Oh, hello,

Doctor!' She smiled and went over to shake him warmly by the hand.

'Say goodbye to Frank and Beryl for me, will you, Ginny?' asked Crispin. 'I'll send them a post-card from Cairo. Oh, and Ginny,' he dipped his hand in his trouser pocket and brought out the white disc, 'I shan't be wanting this again. Mother says I'm not on my own any more. So you have it, Ginny.' Had he not been so young, Virginia would have thought that at that point he deliberately raised his voice to reach Dr Tranter's ears.

'You have it, Ginny,' Crispin repeated in that high carrying voice. 'You haven't got anyone to look after you at all.'

For several moments after Crispin and his mother had gone, Virginia stood staring down at the words on the disc: UNACCOMPANIED. PLEASE HELP. Tears filled her eyes. The words seemed at that moment so very pertinent. She was alone, and she did need help.

Then she felt firm hands on her shoulders, and felt herself spun round.

'Look at me, Virginia.' Richard Tranter put his fingers under her chin and tilted her face so that she was forced to meet his eyes, and their expression as they travelled over her face made her catch her breath.

'So you don't hate me after all?' he asked gently.

She shook her head vehemently. 'Of course not.'

'You certainly gave that impression.'

'I tried to make myself hate you,' she confessed.

'But why . . . *why*?'

'Because I thought you were in love with Clare . . . and I couldn't just feel nothing for you.'

'Oh, my dear!' He hugged her to him. 'Donald is my greatest friend. He asked me to look after her.'

'I know that now,' she murmured.

He held her away from him to study her face again. 'But Peter was different. I thought you were still in love with him.

'That was all over a long time ago,' Virginia assured him.

'Completely?'

'Completely.' She held up the hand that still clutched Crispin's discarded disc.

Smiling, Richard took it from her. 'You won't need this any more either.' His smile deepened. He tore the little disc in pieces as weeks ago he had torn Peter's wedding announcement. 'If you'll let me,' he said humbly, 'I'll accompany you. I want to be with you anywhere and always. Because,' he drew a deep breath and said with a painful catch in his deep slow voice, 'I love you more than anyone and anything else in the world.'

'And I love you.' She felt his arms go tightly round her and his mouth warm and hard on hers. She felt lifted off her feet, carried away, overwhelmed in a wave of unbelievable happiness.

'I should have told you,' Richard said musingly at last, 'when I first realised I loved you.'

'When?' she asked, exploring her happiness.

He sighed. 'I can't remember a time when I didn't love you.' He kissed the top of her head. 'But I did my best to resist.'

'And you didn't succeed?'

'No. I failed miserably.'

She murmured, 'Sometimes you were rather severe and distant . . .'

'Severe with myself, Virginia. Trying hard to keep the relationship professional.' He caught her hand and smiled teasingly. 'With your flair for diagnosis you should have realised that!'

Sister Mortimer, arriving a few minutes later, found Virginia unusually eager to hand over, and Dr Tranter, for the first time in living memory, punctual to leave.

Both those facts were noted by Rosie, who watched Virginia and the Chief walk side by side across the car park to Virginia's faithful old banger. Though neither of them touched the other, she thought she had never seen two people so in love.

She had a bet with herself on wedding bells.

NEW LONGER HISTORICAL ROMANCES

You'll be carried away by The Passionate Pirate.

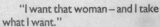

"I want that woman – and I take what I want."

And so the beautiful, headstrong Angelina Blackthorne is abducted by the very man who she held responsible for her father's ruin.

Alone and vulnerable, she falls victim to his ruthless desires.

Yet try as she might, she can't hate him as she feels she should … in the way he so rightly deserves.

'The Passionate Pirate': available from 11th April 1986.

Price £1.50.